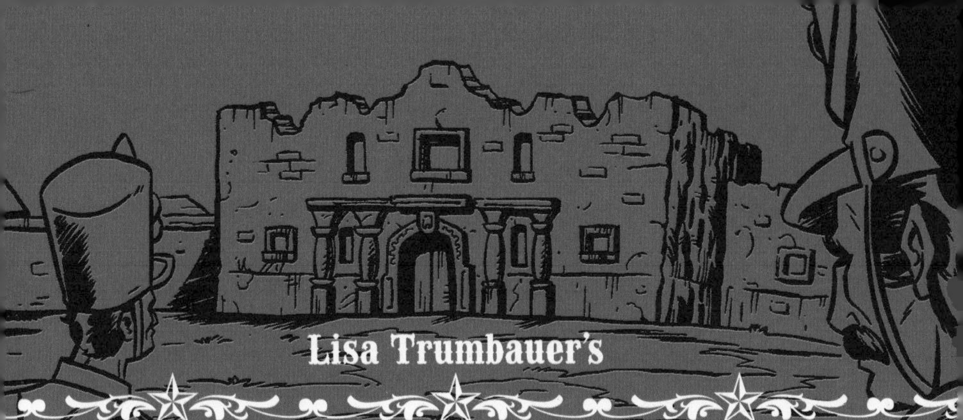

Lisa Trumbauer's

STANDOFF

Remembering the Alamo

illustrated by Brent Schoonover

Librarian Reviewer
Laurie K. Holland
Media Specialist (National Board Certified), Edina, MN
MA in Elementary Education, Minnesota State University, Mankato

Reading Consultant
Elizabeth Stedem
Educator/Consultant, Colorado Springs, CO
MA in Elementary Education, University of Denver, CO

STONE ARCH BOOKS
www.stonearchbooks.com

Graphic Flash is published by Stone Arch Books
151 Good Counsel Drive, P.O. Box 669
Mankato, Minnesota 56002
www.stonearchbooks.com

Library of Congress Cataloging-in-Publication Data
Trumbauer, Lisa, 1963–
Standoff: Remembering the Alamo / by Lisa Trumbauer; illustrated by Brent Schoonover.
p. cm. — (Graphic Flash)
ISBN 978-1-4342-0753-1 (library binding : alk. paper)
ISBN 978-1-4342-0849-1 (pbk. : alk. paper)
1. Graphic novels. [1. Graphic novels. 2. Alamo (San Antonio, Tex.)—Siege, 1836—Fiction. 3. Texas—History—Revolution, 1835–1836—Fiction.] I. Schoonover, Brent, ill. II. Title.
PZ7.7.T78St 2009
[Fic]—dc22 2008006252

Summary: In 1836, 15-year-old Cal and his mother ride across the Texas countryside. Suddenly, they spot thousands of Mexican soldiers approaching on the horizon. Cal knows they mean trouble, so he steers the wagon to the safest place around — the Alamo! Davy Crockett, Jim Bowie, and other soldiers are there, waiting for a fight. But can their small group hold off an entire army? It'll be a battle they'll never forget.

Art Director: Heather Kindseth
Graphic Designer: Brann Garvey

1 2 3 4 5 6 13 12 11 10 09 08

Printed in the United States of America

TABLE OF CONTENTS

INTRODUCING . . .

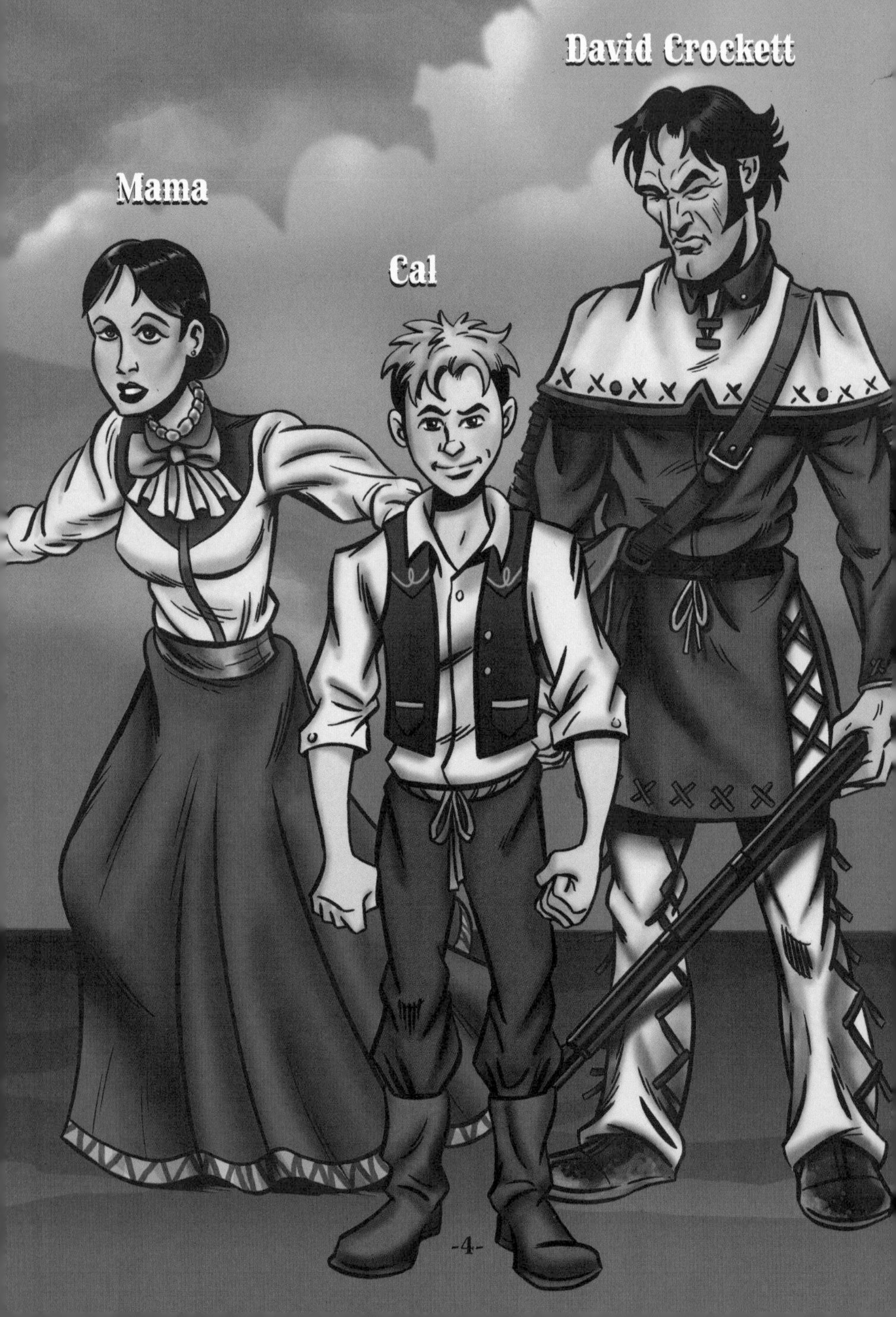
David Crockett
Mama
Cal

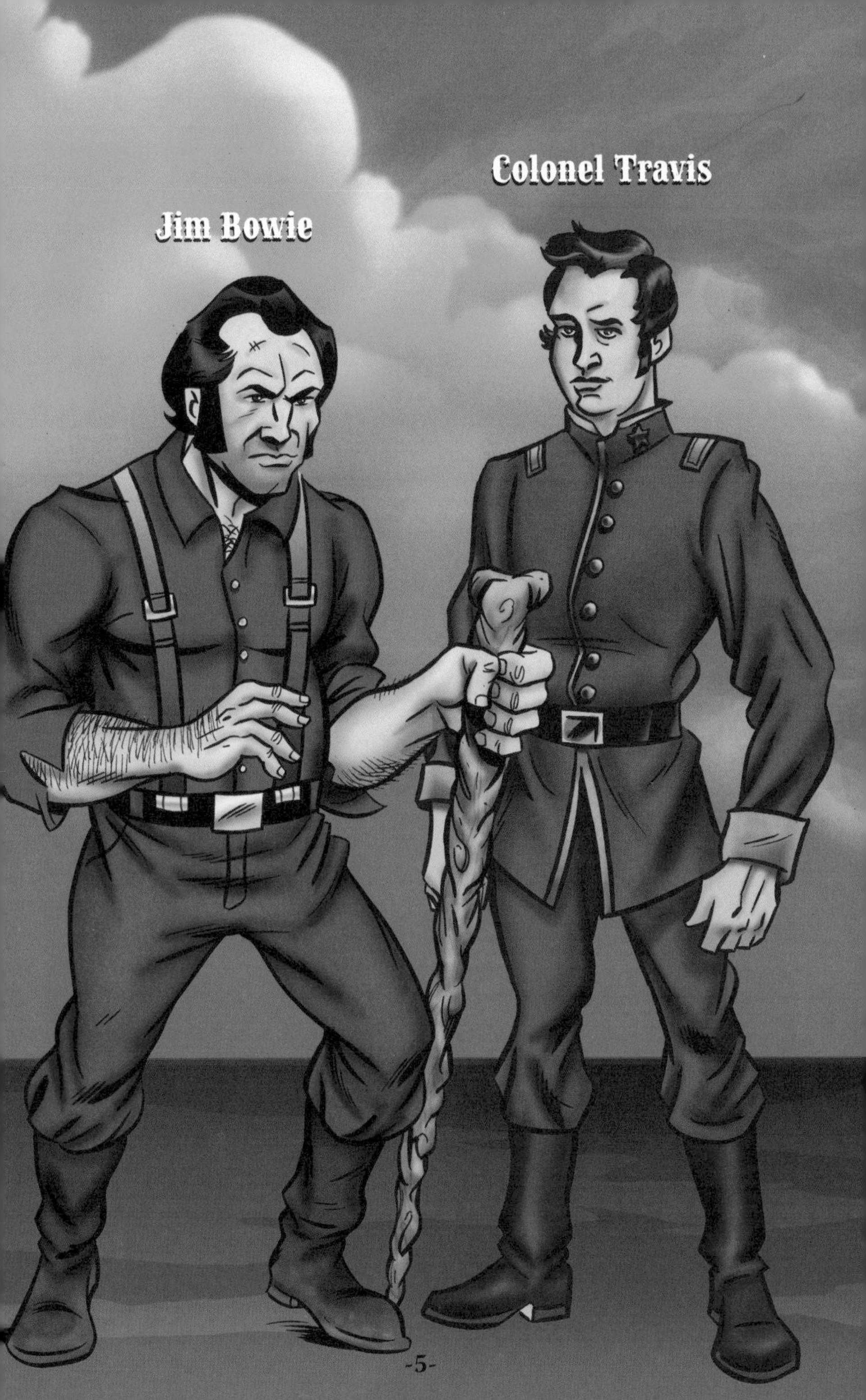
Colonel Travis
Jim Bowie

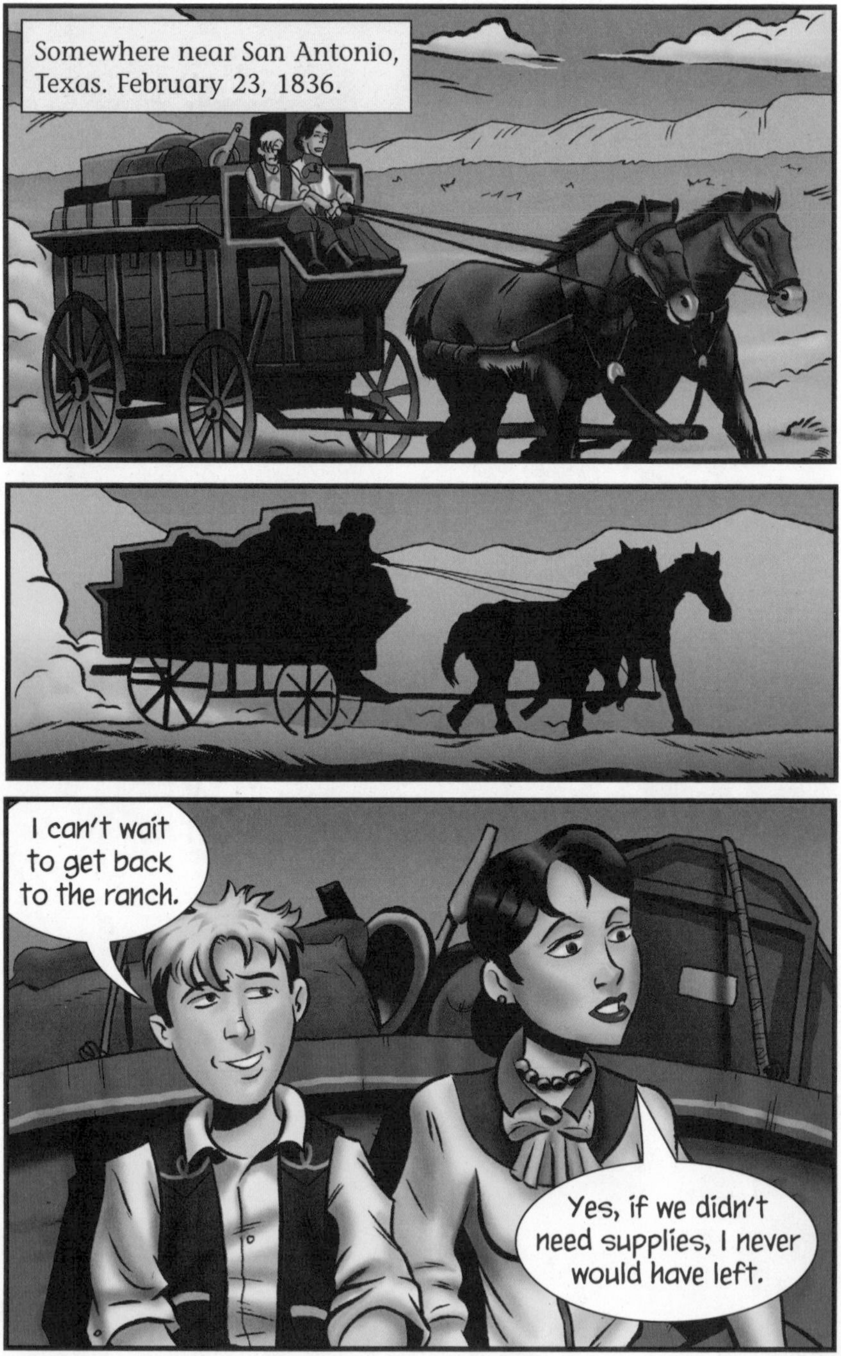
Somewhere near San Antonio, Texas. February 23, 1836.
I can't wait to get back to the ranch.
Yes, if we didn't need supplies, I never would have left.

Chapter 1

ALONE ON THE TRAIL

Cal and his mother continued across the flat Texas landscape. They still had many miles to go before they reached Papa and the ranch. If they were lucky, they would be there by nightfall.

Texas could get very hot, but that February afternoon was unusually cool. Cal's mother wrapped her shawl tightly around her shoulders. She shivered in her seat. Cal could tell that she was nervous.

"It'll be all right, Mama," he said, trying to comfort her. "We're almost home."

His mother nodded, but she was still worried. "I know," she said. "But things are very uncertain in Texas these days."

News spread slowly in Texas, but Cal's mother was well aware of the struggles between Texans and Mexicans. The Mexican army, led by General Santa Anna, wanted Texas to be part of Mexico. Many Americans wanted Texas to be part of the United States. Just two months earlier, in December 1835, Texan troops fought off Mexican soldiers at a battle known as the Siege of Bexar. They had successfully defended an old Spanish mission called the Alamo.

Cal's mother worried that nothing was settled. She worried about her and Cal, alone on the trail.

"It's only been a few months since the Texans fought in San Antonio," she said.

"I heard that battle was glorious!" Cal replied, excitedly. "I wish I could have been there."

"Hush!" his mother snapped. "You should wish no such thing!"

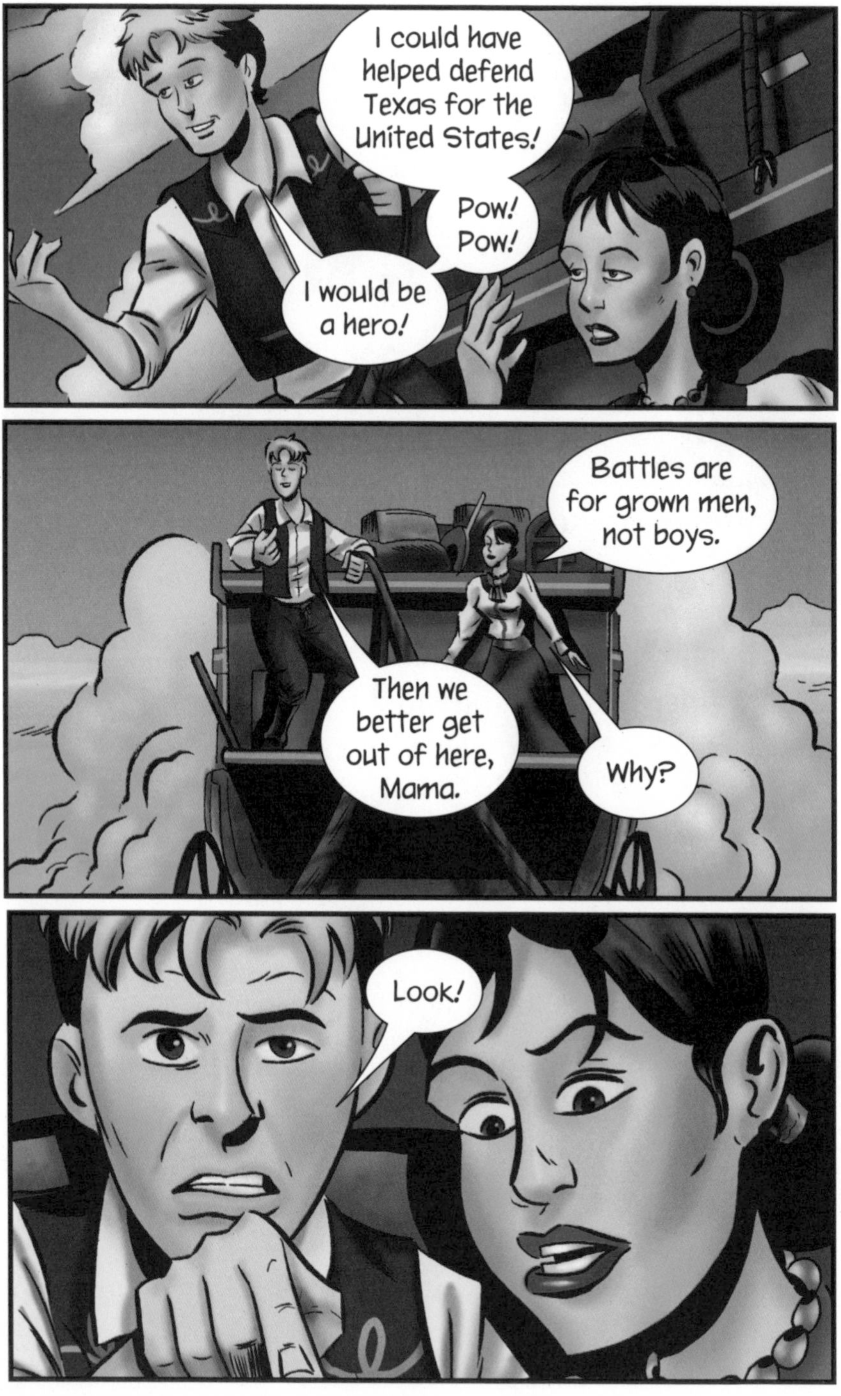
I could have helped defend Texas for the United States!
Pow! Pow!
I would be a hero!
Battles are for grown men, not boys.
Then we better get out of here, Mama.
Why?
Look!

Mama squinted, looking into the distance. At first, she didn't see anything but dust rising off of the ground. Then slowly she made out a thin, dark line. The line appeared to be moving.

"Cal, quick! Turn the cart off the path!" his mother yelled.

"Who are they?" asked Cal.

"I'm not sure, but I don't think we want to be in the open," she said. "We need shelter!"

"Where should we go?" Cal asked his mother.

"We must get to San Antonio," his mother replied. "We'll be safe at the Alamo!"

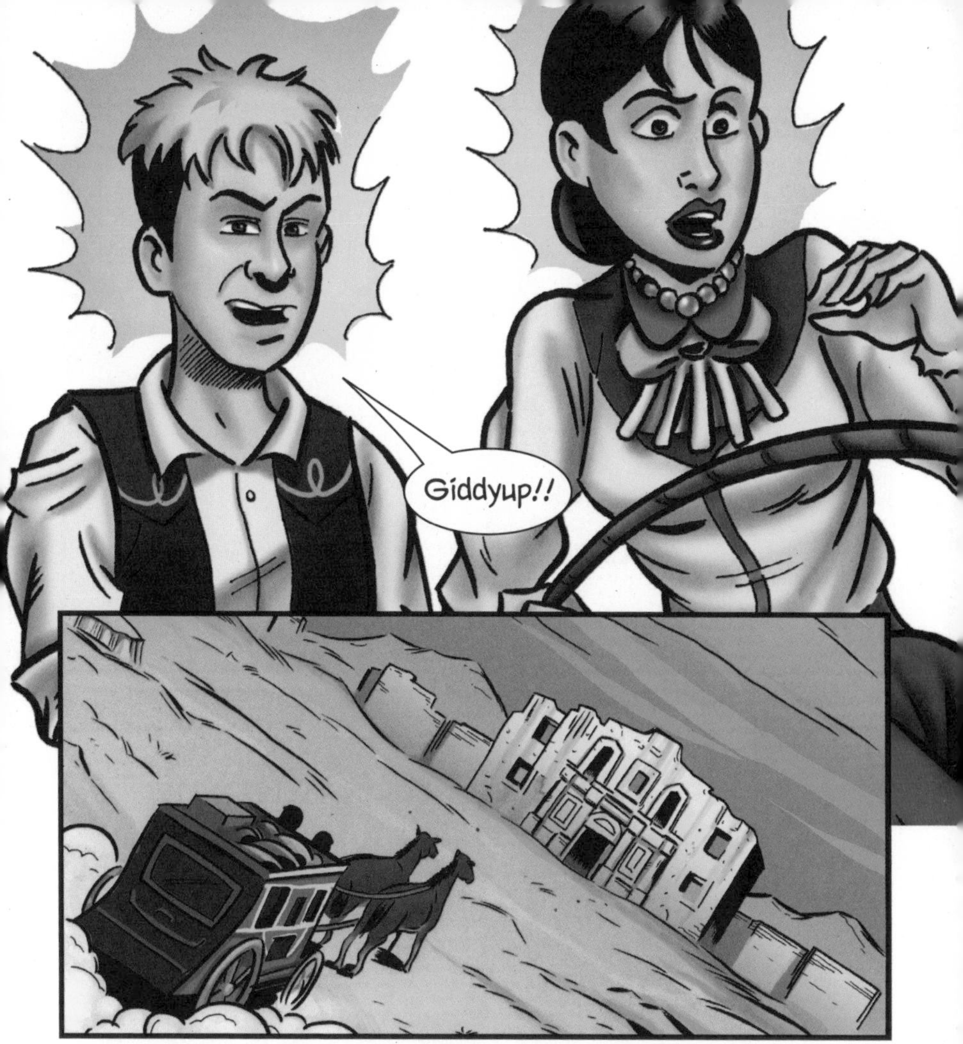
Giddyup!!

Cal and his mother held on tight as the cart bumped over rocks and the wheels spit up dust. The horses snorted, but Cal didn't slow down. He kept his sights fixed on the building in the distance. The walls of white stone guided Cal toward safety.

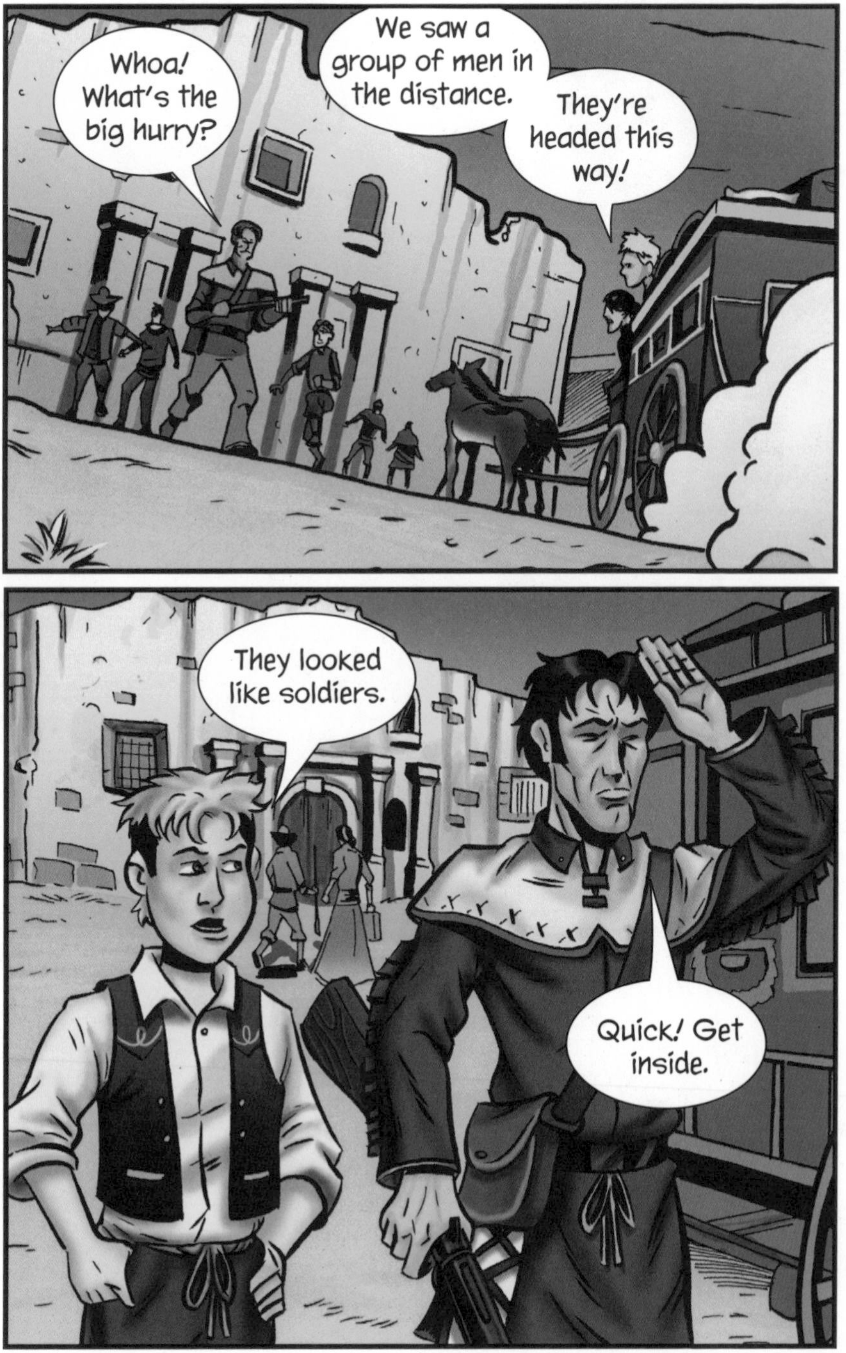
Whoa! What's the big hurry?
We saw a group of men in the distance.
They're headed this way!
They looked like soldiers.
Quick! Get inside.

Chapter 2

TO THE ALAMO

Cal and his mother rushed into the Alamo. They squinted to adjust their eyes to the dim light inside. Cal knew the Alamo had been built as a mission.

He gazed up at the stone walls. It didn't look much like a church at the moment. He didn't see anyone praying. Instead, he saw dozens of men gathered in groups. They were lit by beams of light streaming in from the stone windows. Rifles and long swords lined the walls like soldiers themselves. Pyramids of cannonballs waited in the corners. Dust swirled inside the room, but the space felt cool, almost comforting.

Cal watched as some men sharpened knives or checked their weapons. Others rested against the stone walls, as if storing up energy for later. Still others sat around tables, arguing and discussing. Their voices weren't loud, but they were urgent.

"My name's David Crockett," said the man who led them inside. "Thank you both for the warning."

"Is it the Mexicans, Mr. Crockett?" Cal asked.

"We can only hope not, Cal," said his mother, looking worried.

"Your mother's right," said Crockett. "But I have a feeling that we're about to find out otherwise."

Just then, Cal felt a rumbling beneath his feet. He heard a noise that sounded like distant thunder. Many of the soldiers inside the Alamo rose to their feet.

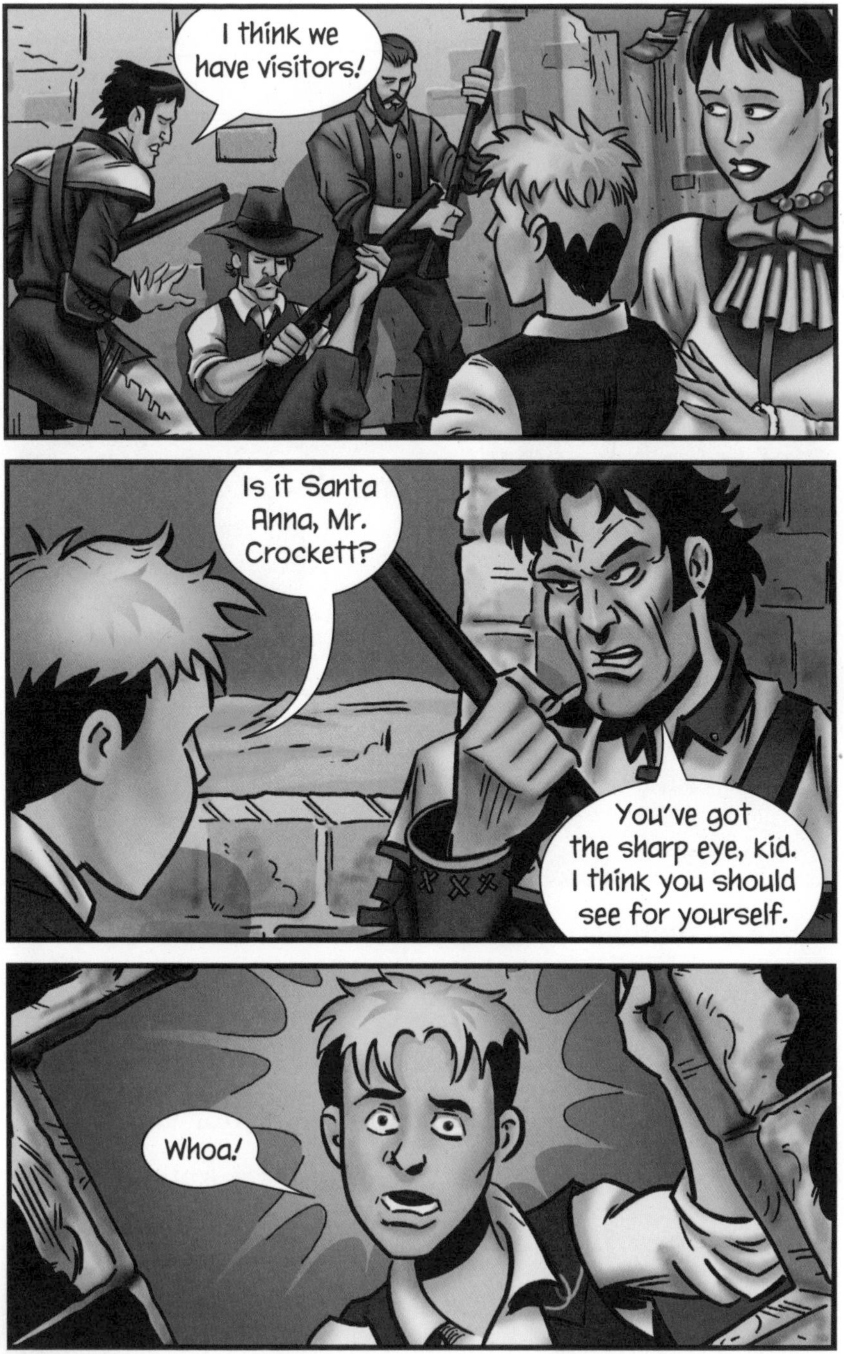
I think we have visitors!
Is it Santa Anna, Mr. Crockett?
You've got the sharp eye, kid. I think you should see for yourself.
Whoa!

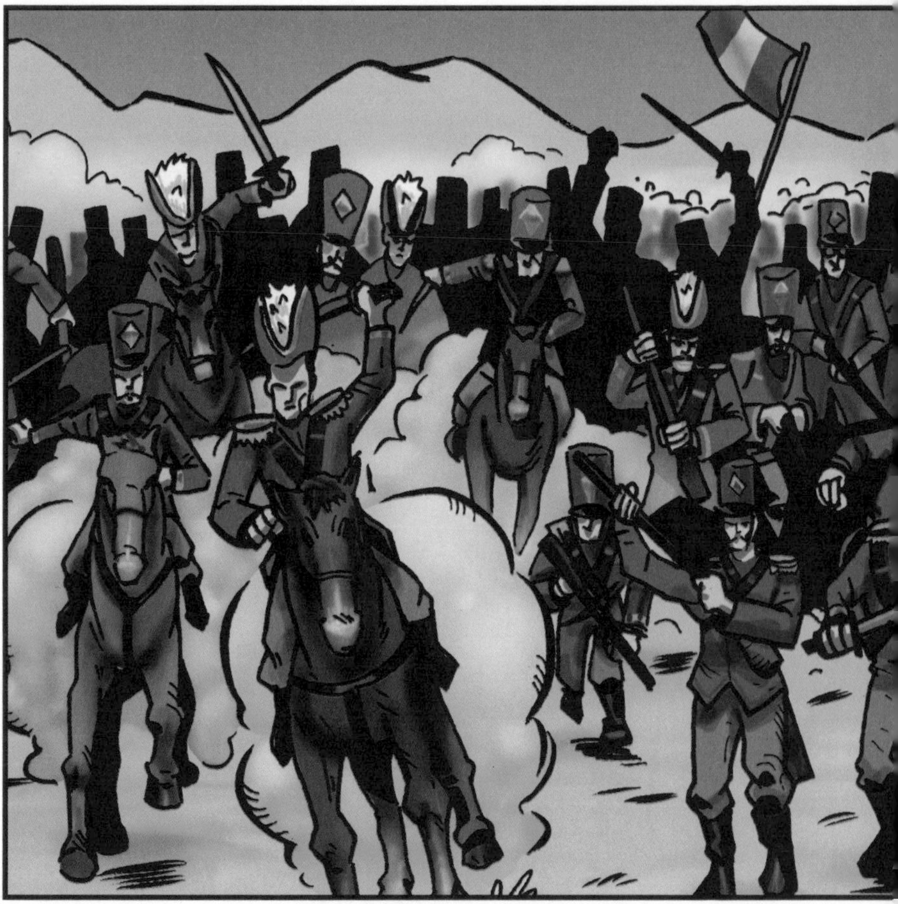

Cal watched from the window as the Mexican army advanced. Their line stretched as far as he could see. Cal thought he counted hundreds, no thousands, of soldiers. Some rode on horseback. Others marched on foot. Several of the soldiers rode horses that pulled huge cannons. They were all headed toward the Alamo.

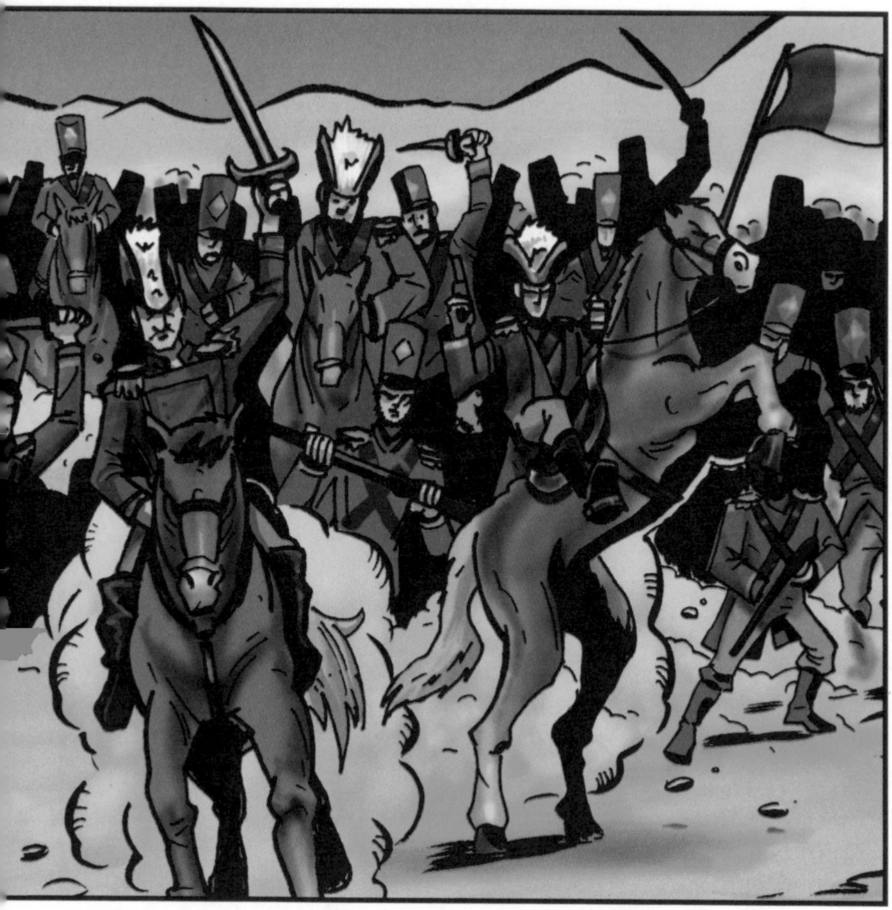

Their footsteps and horses churned up the earth into dusty clouds. Cal could hear their Spanish voices, the jingle of their weapons, and the pounding hooves of their horses. It was like a giant dust storm had blown in from the south, and it was bent on destroying them. Suddenly, all of the soldiers stopped, except for one.

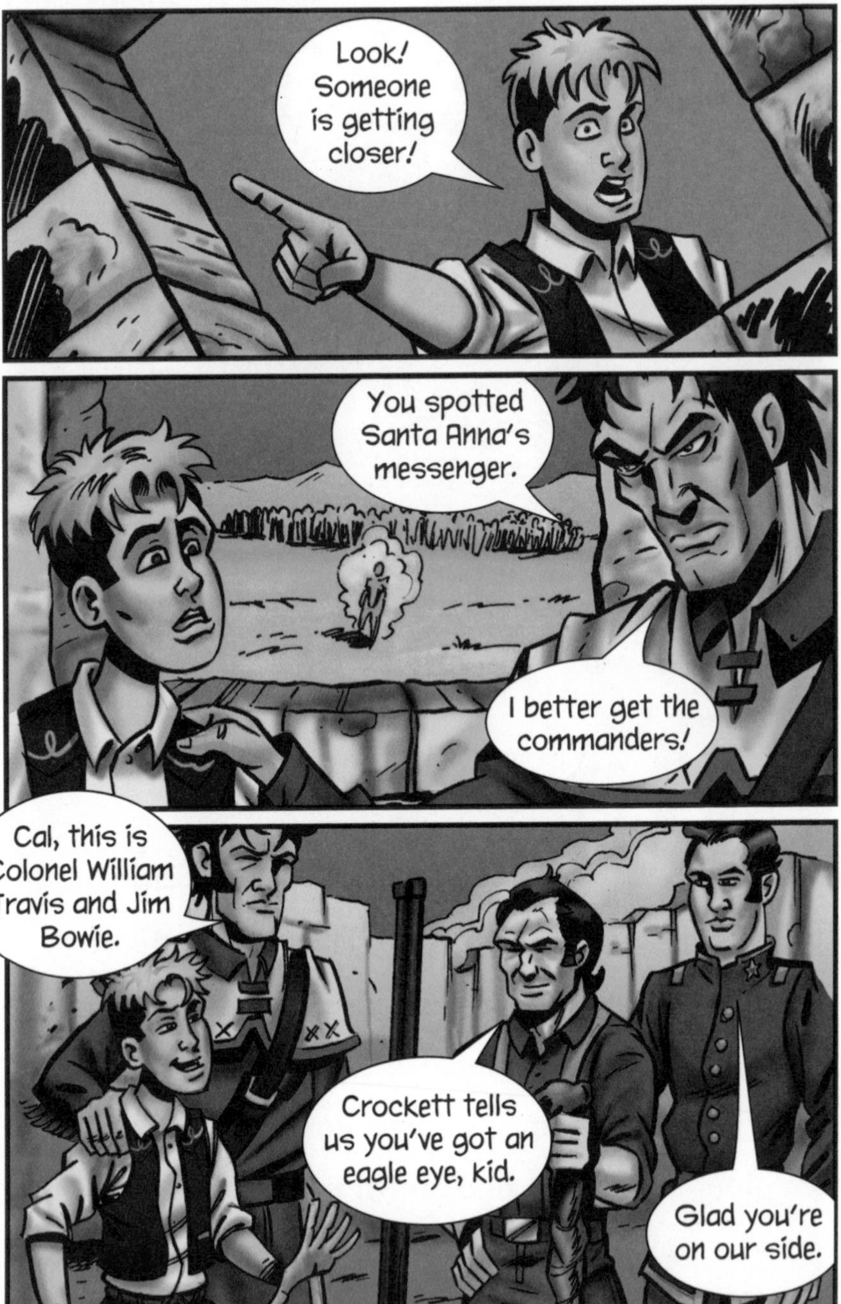
Look! Someone is getting closer!
You spotted Santa Anna's messenger.
I better get the commanders!
Cal, this is Colonel William Travis and Jim Bowie.
Crockett tells us you've got an eagle eye, kid.
Glad you're on our side.

Cal watched in awe as Crockett and the commanders exited the Alamo. Through the window, he saw three men discuss the message. They shook their heads and even laughed a bit, but Cal didn't think they were happy.

Cal was worried. The Mexican army outside was huge. He looked around the Alamo, and he knew they were outnumbered. He'd only seen a few dozen men inside. He was sure more had gathered in other areas of the mission. But could a hundred men fight against thousands?

Cal glanced up at the stone walls of the Alamo. *The Alamo is strong enough to keep us safe,* he thought. Cal wished he could hear what the men were talking about. He didn't want them to surrender, even if the odds were against them.

"I'm going to find out what's happening," he said. Before his mother could stop him, Cal ran toward the Alamo door.

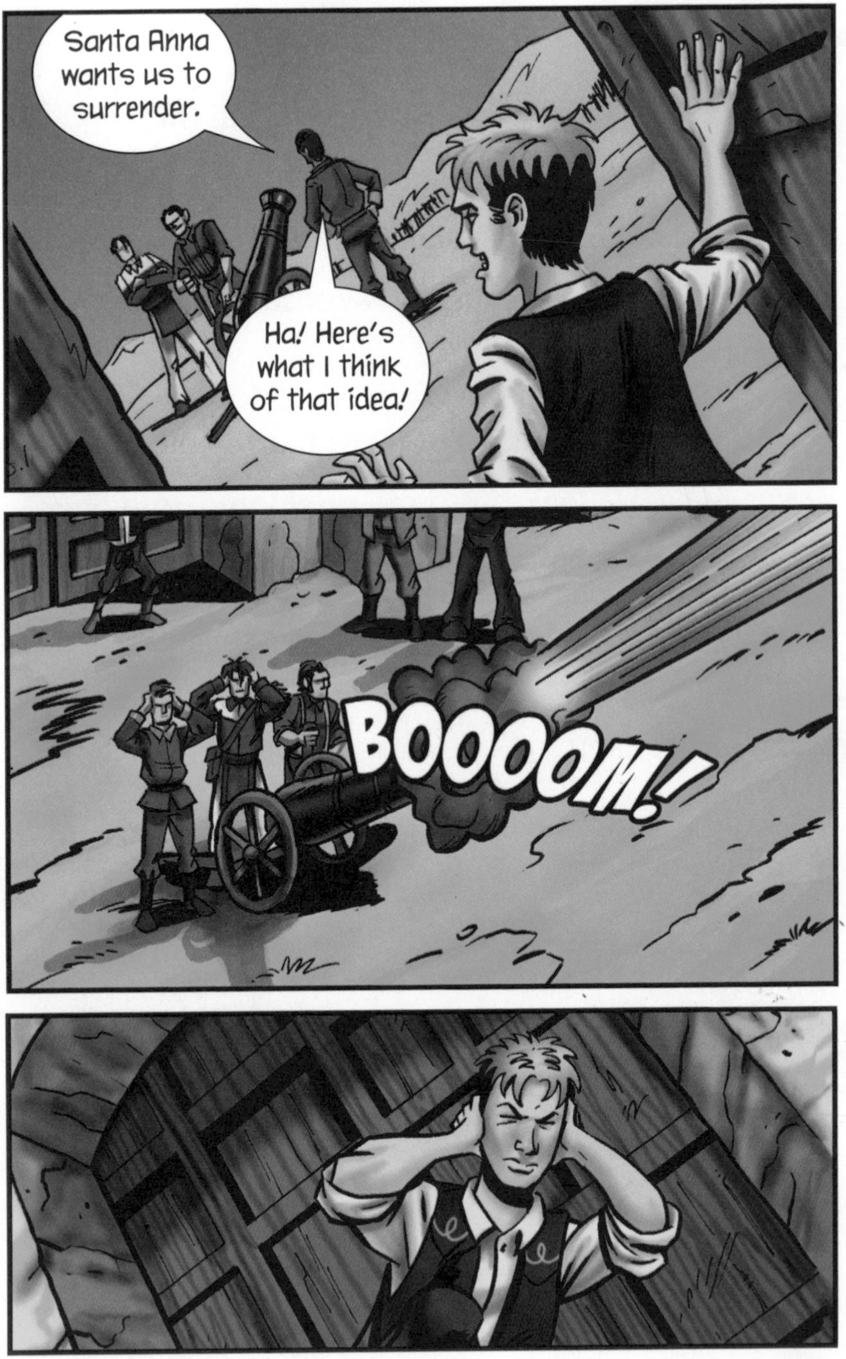
Santa Anna wants us to surrender.
Ha! Here's what I think of that idea!
BOOOOM!

After the powerful blast, the air was silent. No one inside the mission spoke. No bird outside the mission sang. Even the horses outside seemed to be holding their breath.

After a moment, a few men started to cheer. Then, Cal worked up the courage to yell out.

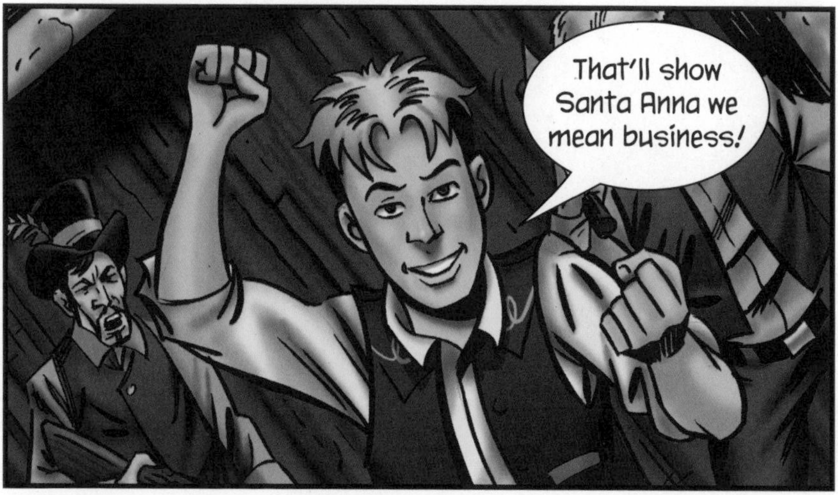
That'll show Santa Anna we mean business!

In all of the excitement, Cal barely heard the cannon blasts erupting from the Mexican army. In the distance, he spotted a small puff of smoke. Then he saw another and another. The Mexican army had begun its own attack.

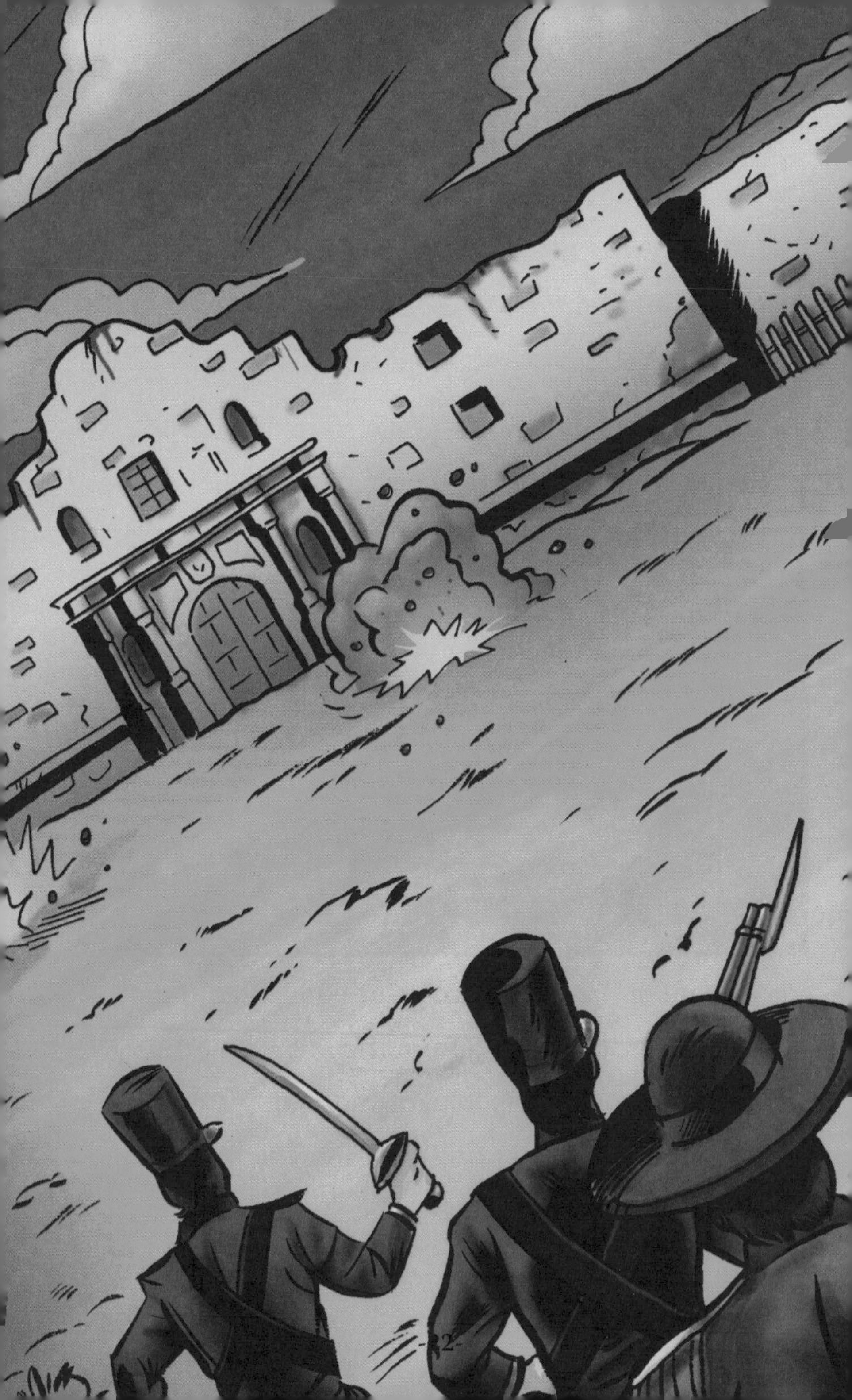

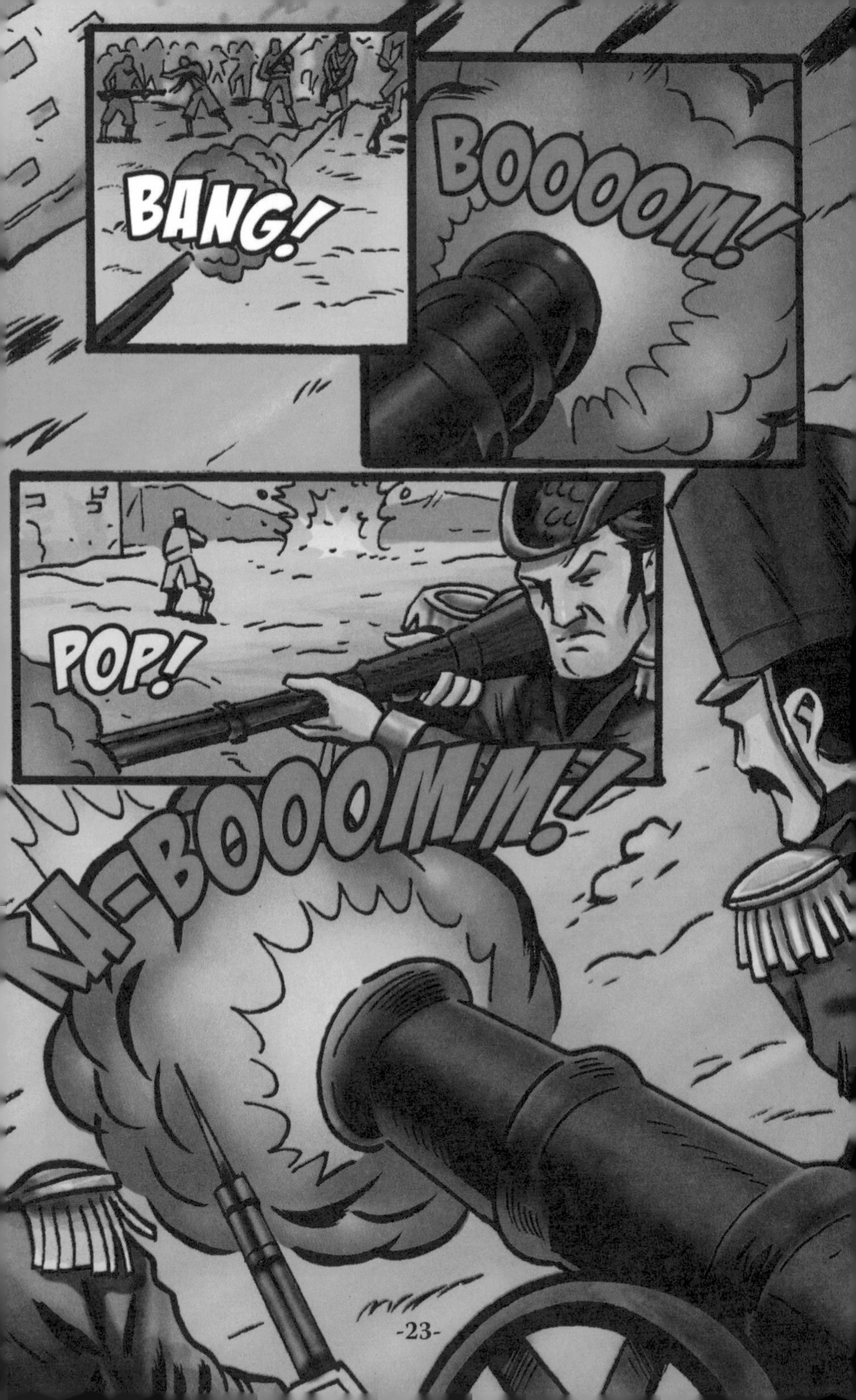
BANG!
BOOOOOM!
POP!
KA-BOOOMM!

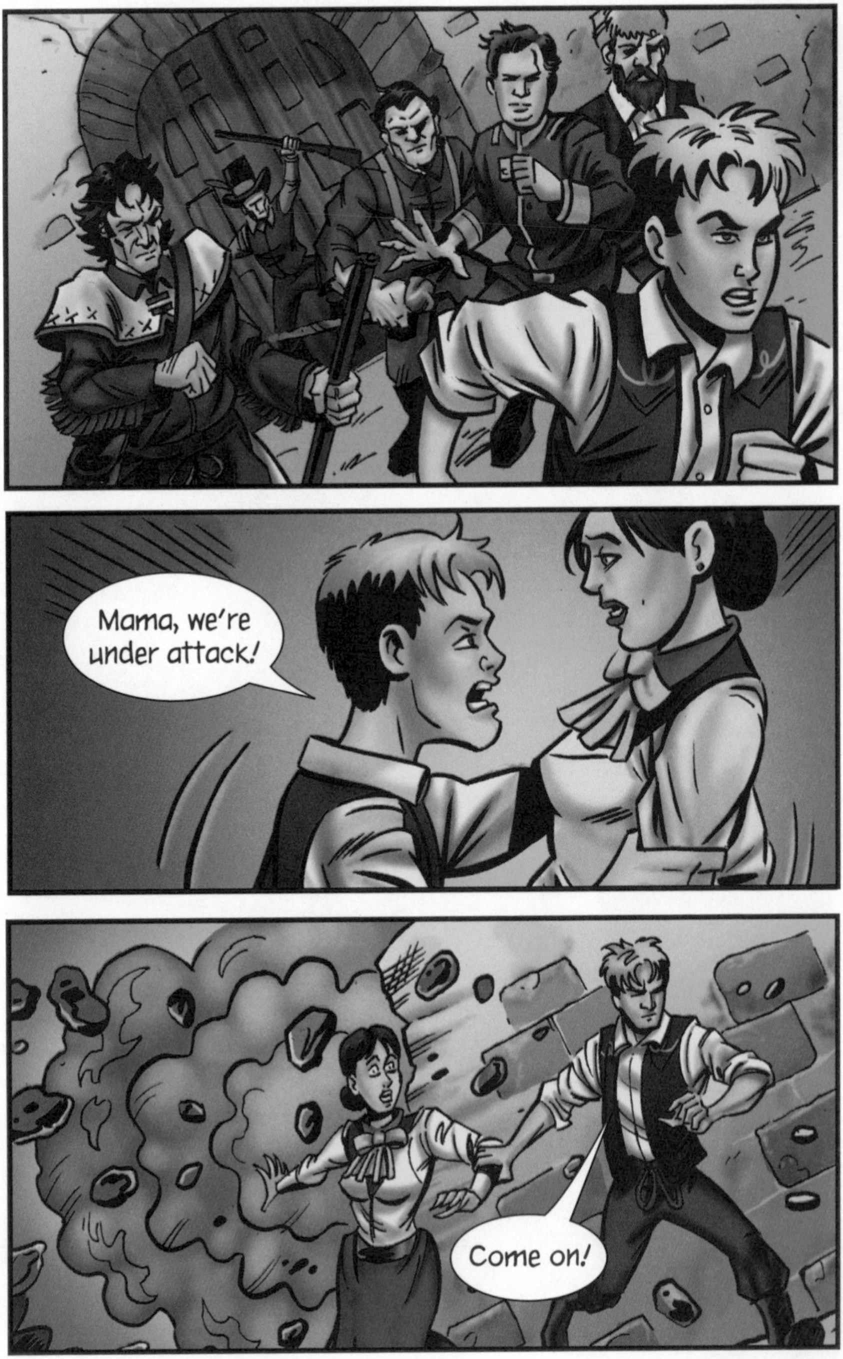
Mama, we're under attack!
Come on!

Cal led his mother deeper into the Alamo. He wanted to find a place where the bullets and cannonballs wouldn't reach them. As they ran, the ground continued to shake with explosions. All around, they saw groups of soldiers with guns grasped in their hands, uncertain what to do. Cal wondered what to do as well.

Finally, Cal and his mother stopped. They sat and rested in the safest spot they could find.

"When will they stop shooting, Mama?" Cal asked, trying to catch his breath.

"They're hoping we'll surrender," she replied.

"Why don't we fight back?" he asked.

Cal didn't think a real soldier would run and hide. He started to stand up, and then felt a hand grasp his shoulder.

"Mr. Crockett!" Cal shouted, surprised.

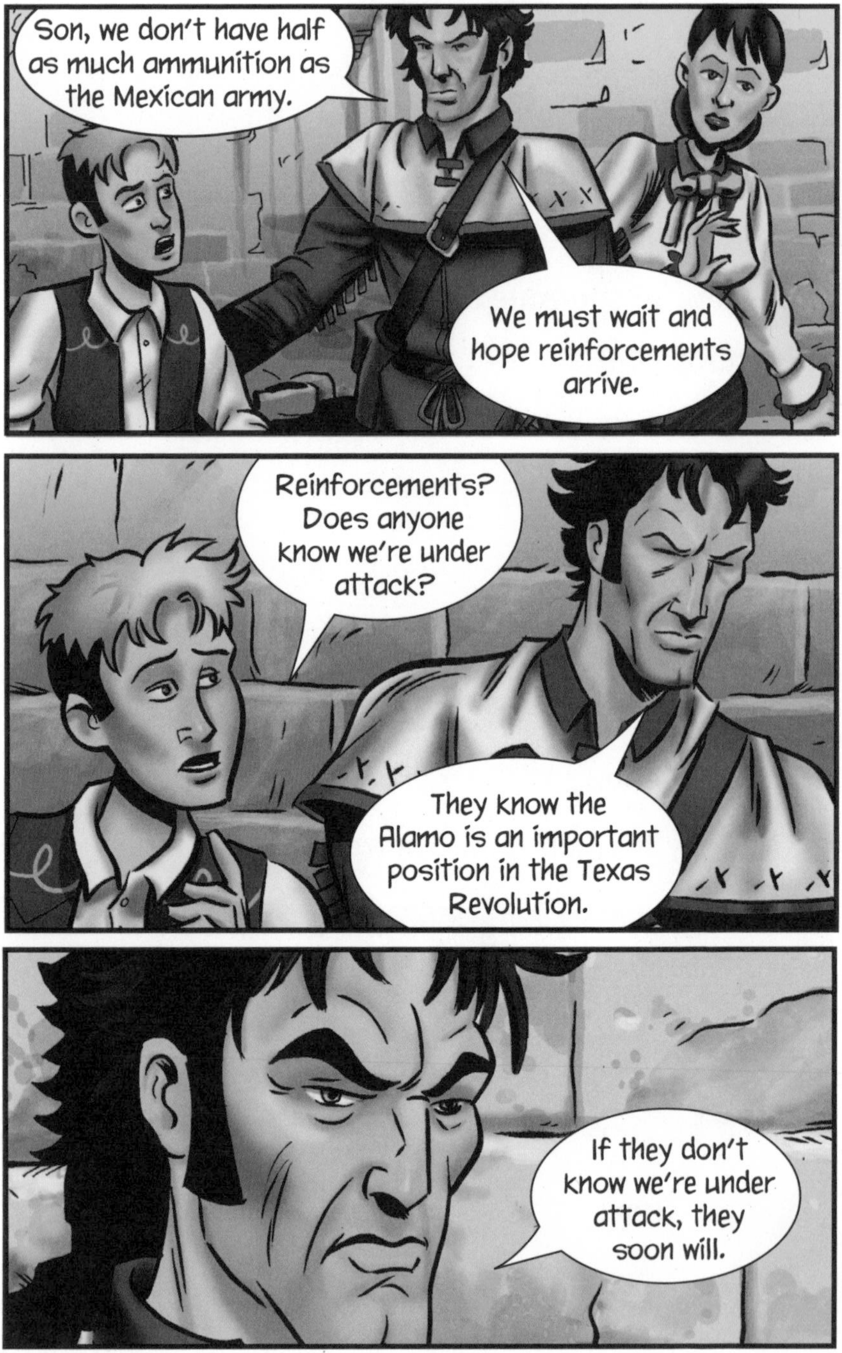
Son, we don't have half as much ammunition as the Mexican army.
We must wait and hope reinforcements arrive.
Reinforcements? Does anyone know we're under attack?
They know the Alamo is an important position in the Texas Revolution.
If they don't know we're under attack, they soon will.

Chapter 3

WAITING FOR HELP

Cal thought he'd get used to the explosions, but he didn't. The Mexican army continued firing all day. Cal and his mother huddled with the rest of the men, listening to the cannonballs smash sections of the Alamo. A few other women and children also had taken shelter at the Alamo. Mama talked with the women. They all kept an eye on their children.

Cal was nervous. He didn't want to leave his mother, but he had to know what was going on. He followed Mr. Crockett and Colonel Travis around the old mission. He learned that Jim Bowie was feeling poorly and was not able to lead as he had hoped. That meant Colonel Travis was in charge.

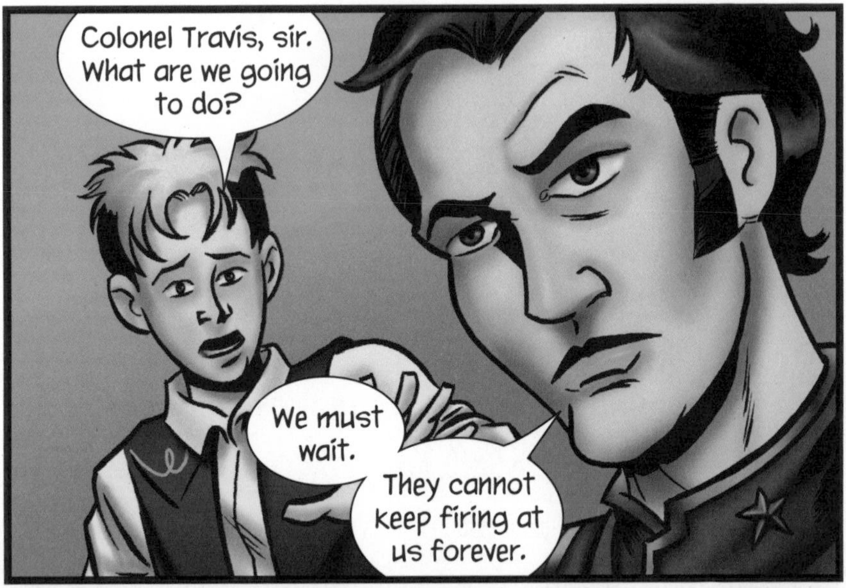
Colonel Travis, sir. What are we going to do?
We must wait.
They cannot keep firing at us forever.

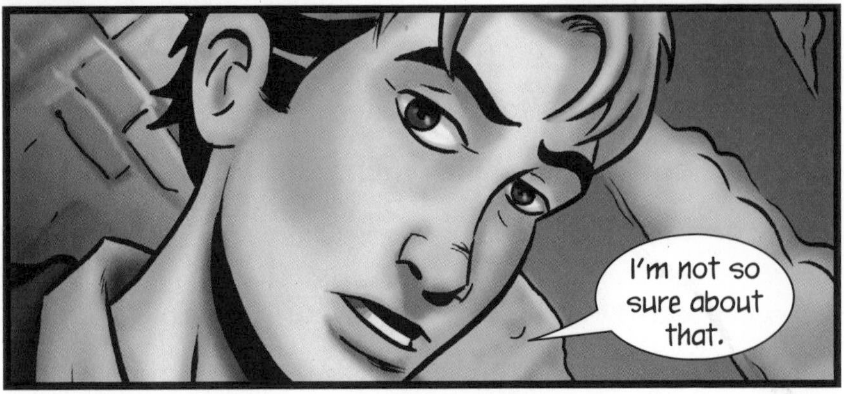
I'm not so sure about that.

The explosion didn't end with nightfall. Cal thought it would be impossible to sleep through the rumbling, but he was tired. What finally woke him was the quiet the next morning. The Alamo had been under siege for nearly 24 hours.

The soldiers inside the fort had barely slept. Cal and his mother had slept on the hard, dirt floor. They shared a single blanket with other women and children trapped inside.

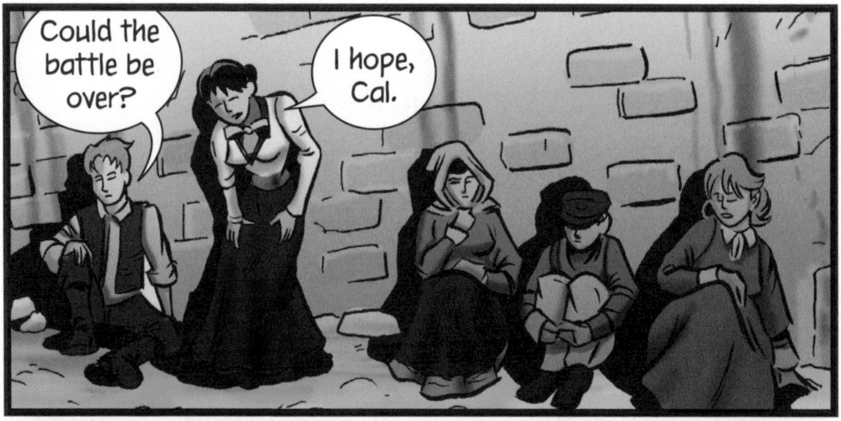
Could the battle be over?
I hope, Cal.

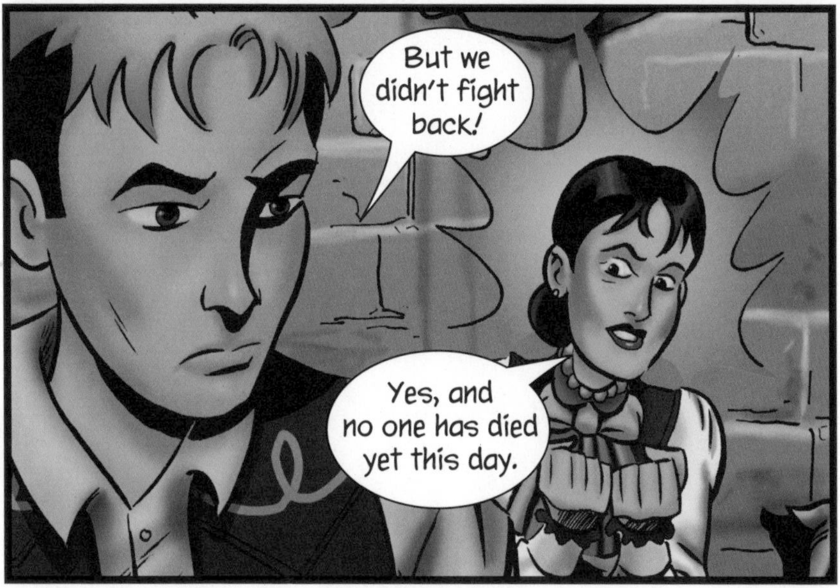
But we didn't fight back!
Yes, and no one has died yet this day.

Cal jumped up and ran to a window. Looking out, he could see the Mexican army. They hadn't retreated or given up. Cal got the feeling that they were waiting for something. Did they want a fight or a surrender?

He ran through the mission, looking for Colonel Travis or Mr. Crockett. On the way, he passed Jim Bowie, who was lying on a cot. Mr. Bowie coughed, and Cal realized he wouldn't be much help if the Mexicans stormed the Alamo. Mr. Bowie was ill and very weak. That meant one less man to fight for the Texans.

Cal continued through the mission. Finally, he spotted Colonel Travis, sitting alone and writing.

"Why is it so quiet, sir?" Cal asked.

"I suppose they're giving us a chance to rethink our position," said Colonel Travis, continuing to write.

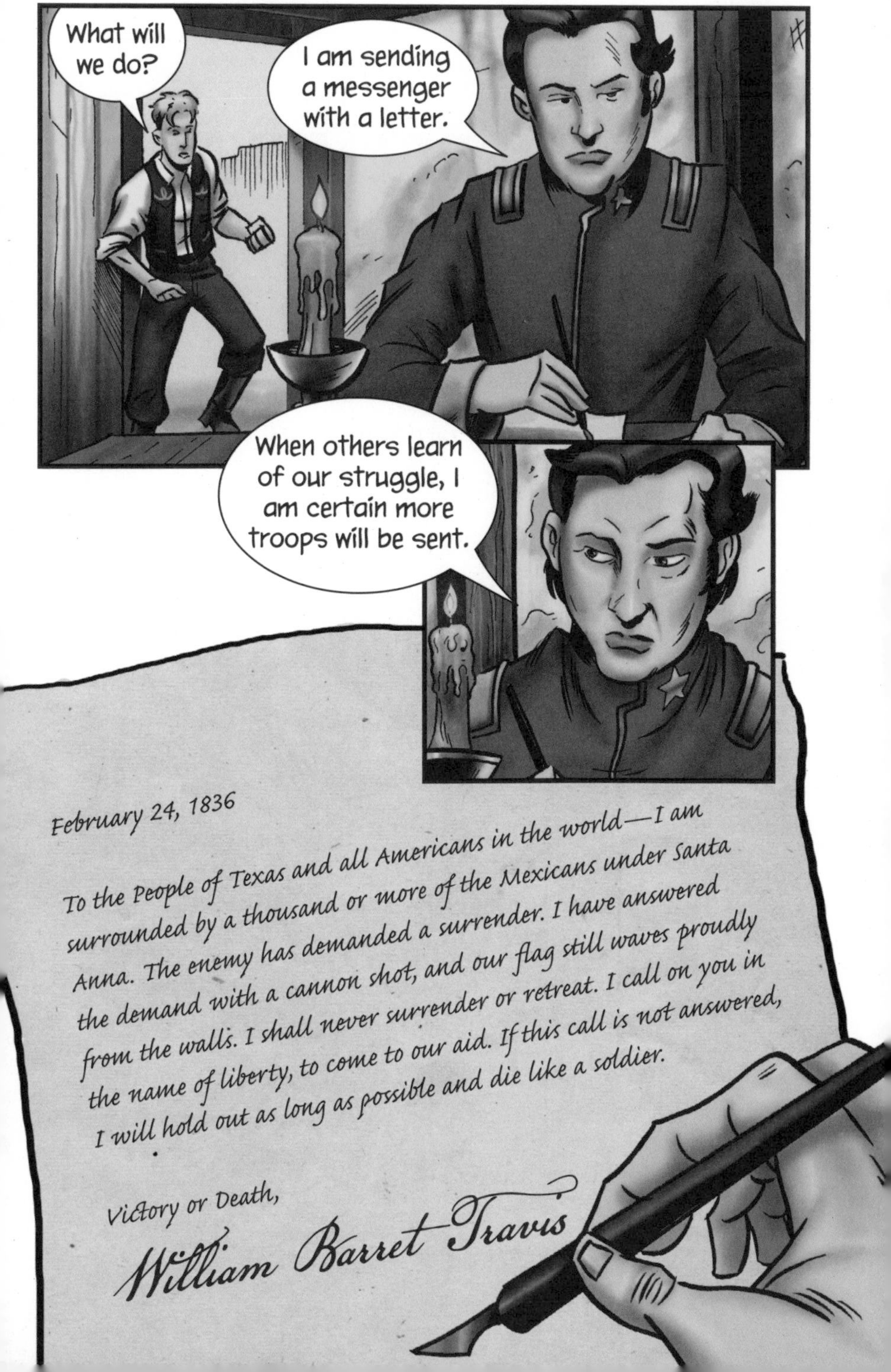
What will we do?
I am sending a messenger with a letter.
When others learn of our struggle, I am certain more troops will be sent.
February 24, 1836
To the People of Texas and all Americans in the world—I am surrounded by a thousand or more of the Mexicans under Santa Anna. The enemy has demanded a surrender. I have answered the demand with a cannon shot, and our flag still waves proudly from the walls. I shall never surrender or retreat. I call on you in the name of liberty, to come to our aid. If this call is not answered, I will hold out as long as possible and die like a soldier.
Victory or Death,
William Barret Travis

Chapter 4

REINFORCEMENTS

All was quiet for the next few days. As Cal walked among the soldiers, he heard plans and strategies about how to defend the Alamo. He heard heated talks about the rights of Americans and the rights of Mexicans. He also noticed the weariness of the soldiers. Food supplies were running low. He and his mother only ate small bits of bread and cheese each day. Cal wondered how the soldiers could keep up their strength.

Cal watched the Mexican army from one of the stone windows. They were camped in plain view, yet they did not attack. *Maybe they're trying to starve us out,* he thought.

Cal turned toward his mother, who was laying nearby and looking weak. "How are you holding up, Mama?" he asked.

"I'm just tired," she said. "Cal, what do you think will happen to us?"

Cal was surprised his mother was asking him this question. Usually, she had all of the answers.

"I think more troops will arrive," Cal replied, remembering what Colonel Travis had told him. "I don't think the United States wants the Alamo and San Antonio to fall to the Mexican army."

"How long will it take?" his mother asked. "I can't imagine how worried your papa must be."

"Hopefully not too much longer," Cal said, glancing back toward the window. "We don't have much food or water left."

Suddenly, Cal spotted movement in the distance. He knew exactly what it was.

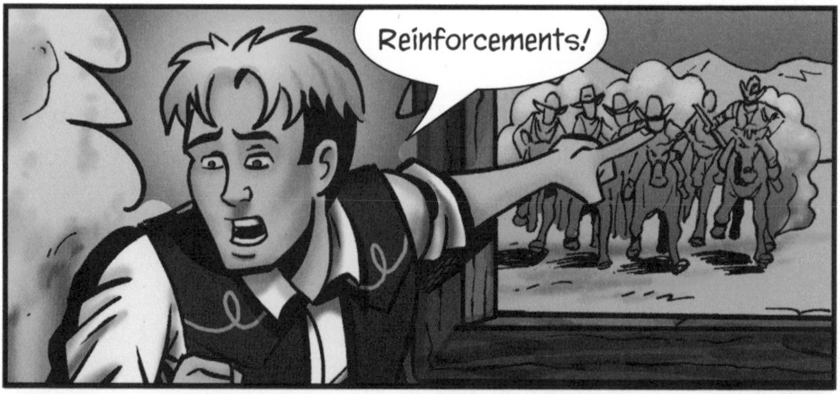
Reinforcements!

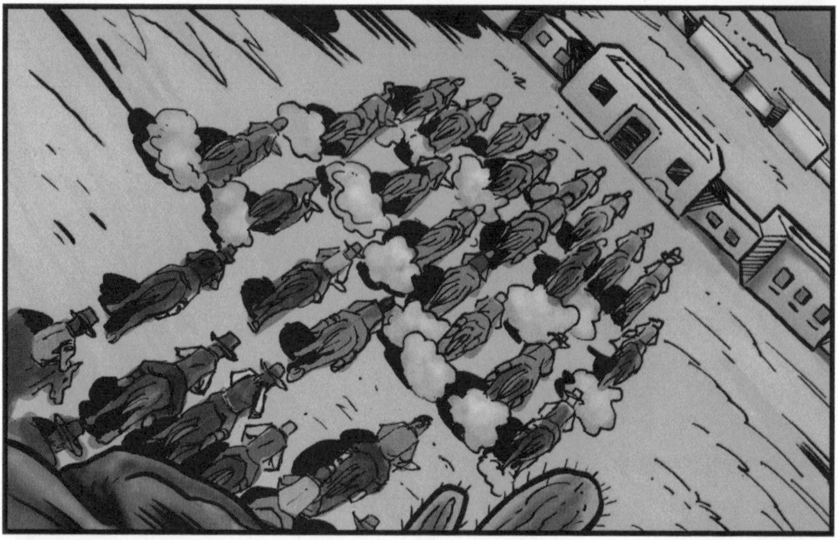

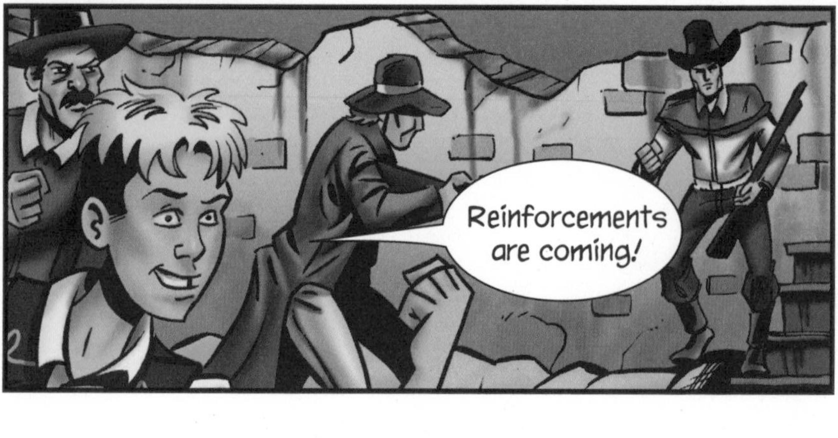
Reinforcements are coming!

Cal followed Colonel Travis outside. He wanted to greet the new soldiers too.

"Only 32 men?!" shouted Colonel Travis. He stared at the group of reinforcements. "We're facing thousands!"

Cal couldn't believe it either. Like the rest of the Alamo soldiers, he thought hundreds of troops would arrive. Right then, Cal decided he had to help. He was good with a gun, but he didn't know if he could actually use it against another person. He could help with loading ammunition, though.

That night, Cal borrowed a soldier's rifle. He practiced reloading the gun over and over again. He also talked to some of the soldiers about the cannons. He learned how to stuff the cannonballs into the long iron tube. He helped the soldiers pile up cannonballs and supplies for when the time came to use them.

Chapter 5

UNDER ATTACK!

Keeping busy helped the days pass more quickly, but not quickly enough. Cal began to lose count of how many days it had been. A week? Two weeks? The Mexican army continued to grow outside. More men appeared on horseback. More weapons arrived. Cal thought the Mexican army was like a giant bug, one that kept growing and would eventually eat up everything in its path.

"This can't last forever," Cal said to his mother. "We have only about 200 men. Two hundred men cannot hold back thousands of soldiers."

"Try to rest, Cal," she said, looking up at her son. "Tomorrow is another day."

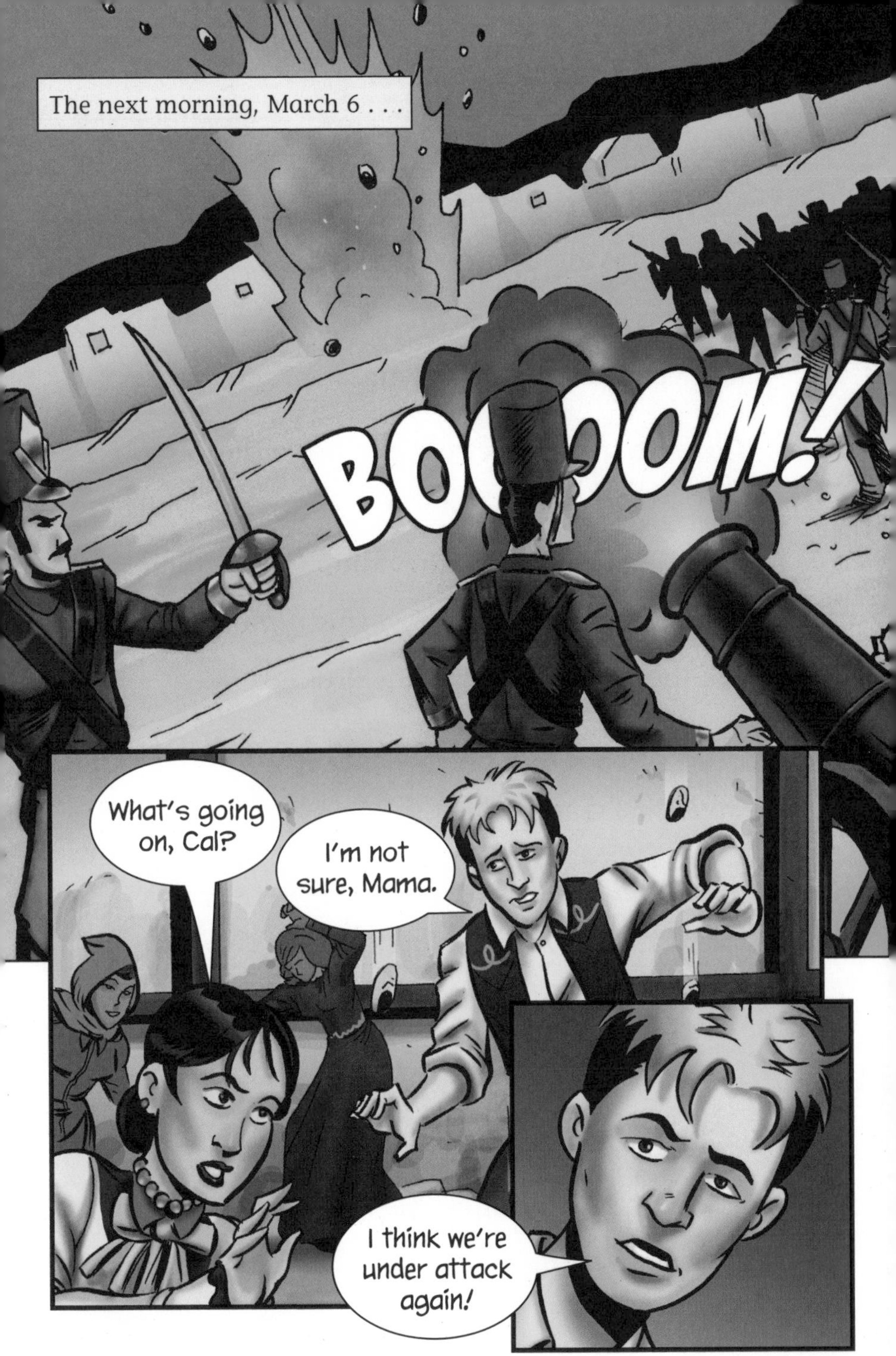

The next morning, March 6 . . .
BOOOOOM!
What's going on, Cal?
I'm not sure, Mama.
I think we're under attack again!

Cal flew through the mission. Everywhere, men were taking up arms and loading cannons. Shots rang out, cannons boomed, and shouts of victory echoed through the mission.

Cal watched as the soldiers inside the Alamo fought and defended the fort. Even as the walls around them exploded, they didn't leave their weapons. Then suddenly, Cal saw a man near one of the cannons fall to the ground.

"You!" another soldier yelled toward Cal. "Help me load this cannon!"

For a moment, Cal wondered if the soldier was really pointing at him. When no one else stepped forward, Cal decided this was his chance.

"Yes, sir," he replied.

Cal started passing cannonballs to the soldier. After only a few minutes, his arms ached, but he refused to give up.

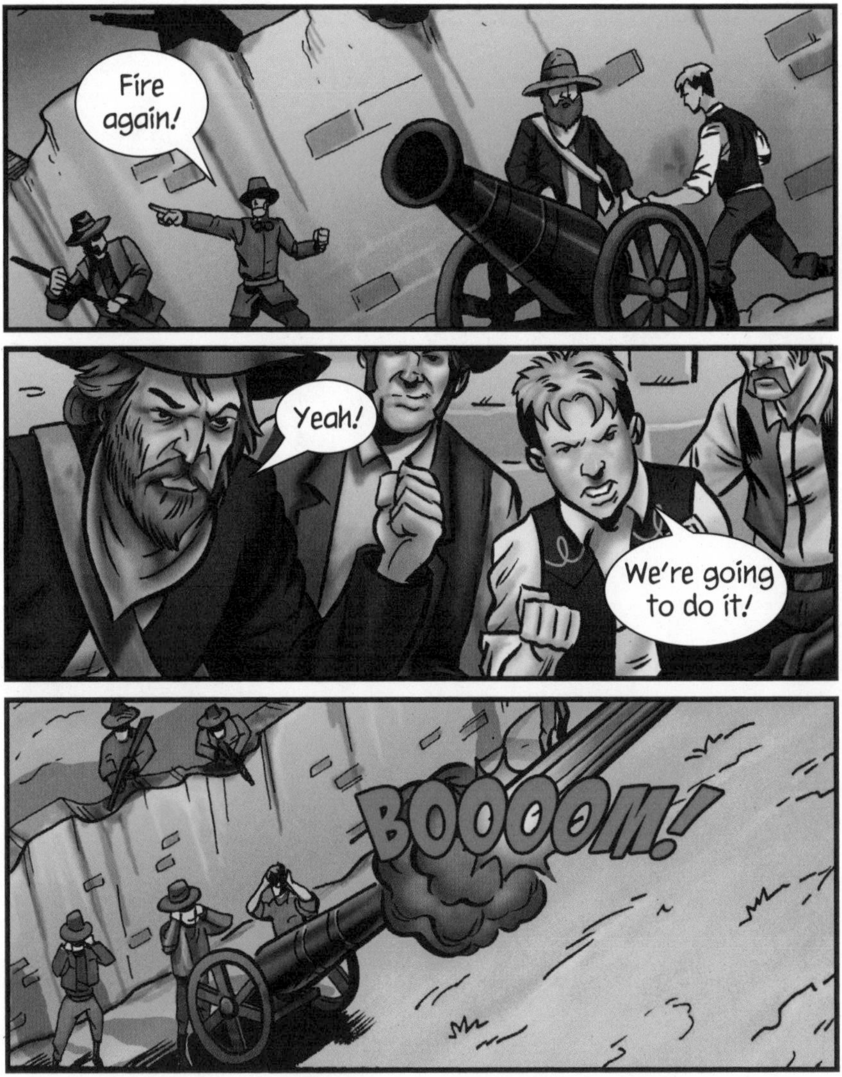
Fire again!
Yeah!
We're going to do it!
BOOOOM!

Peering over the stone wall of the Alamo, Cal watched as Mexican soldiers fell. Their plan seemed to be working. Behind the walls of the Alamo, the Mexican army couldn't reach them.

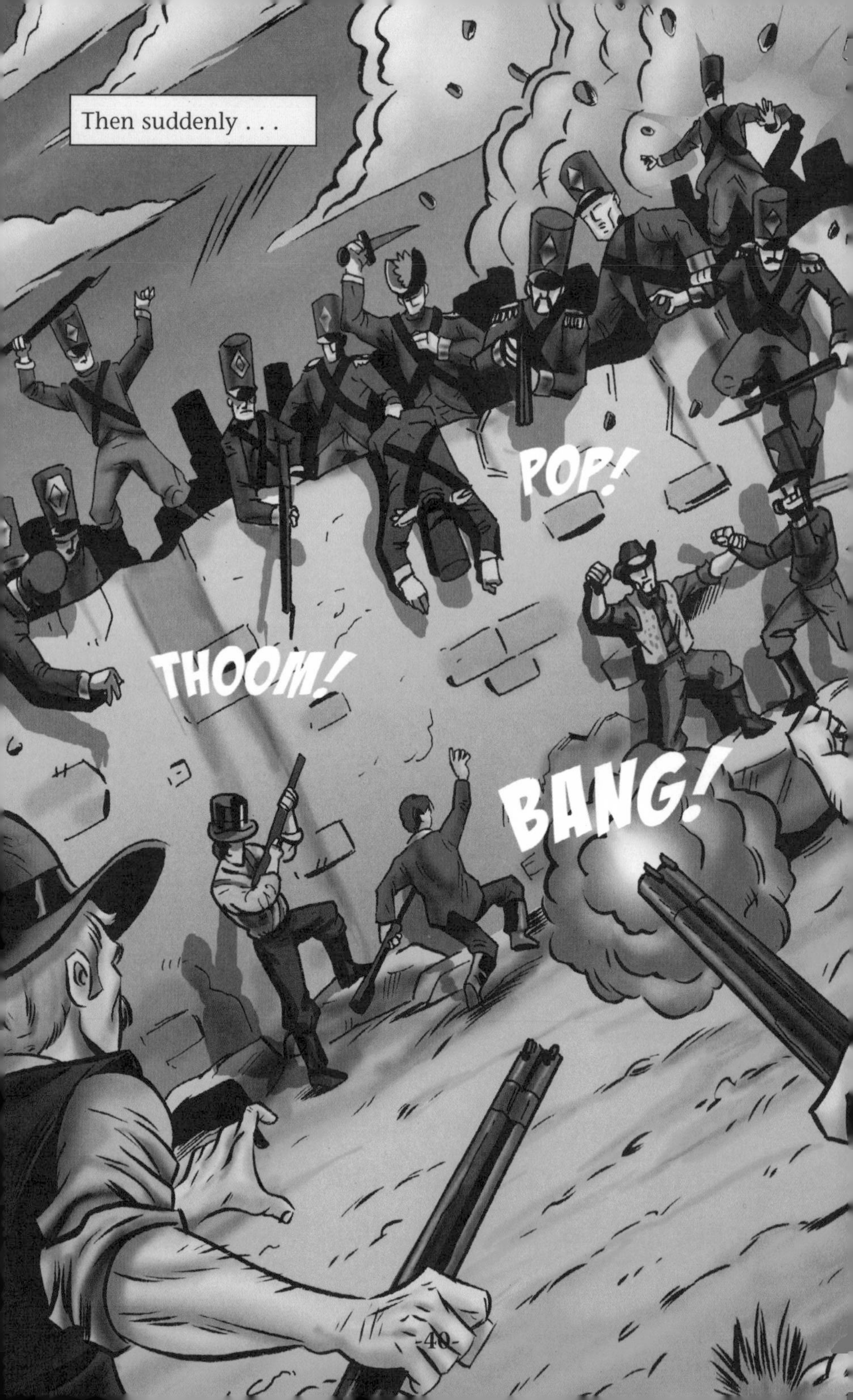
Then suddenly . . .
POP!
THOOM!
BANG!

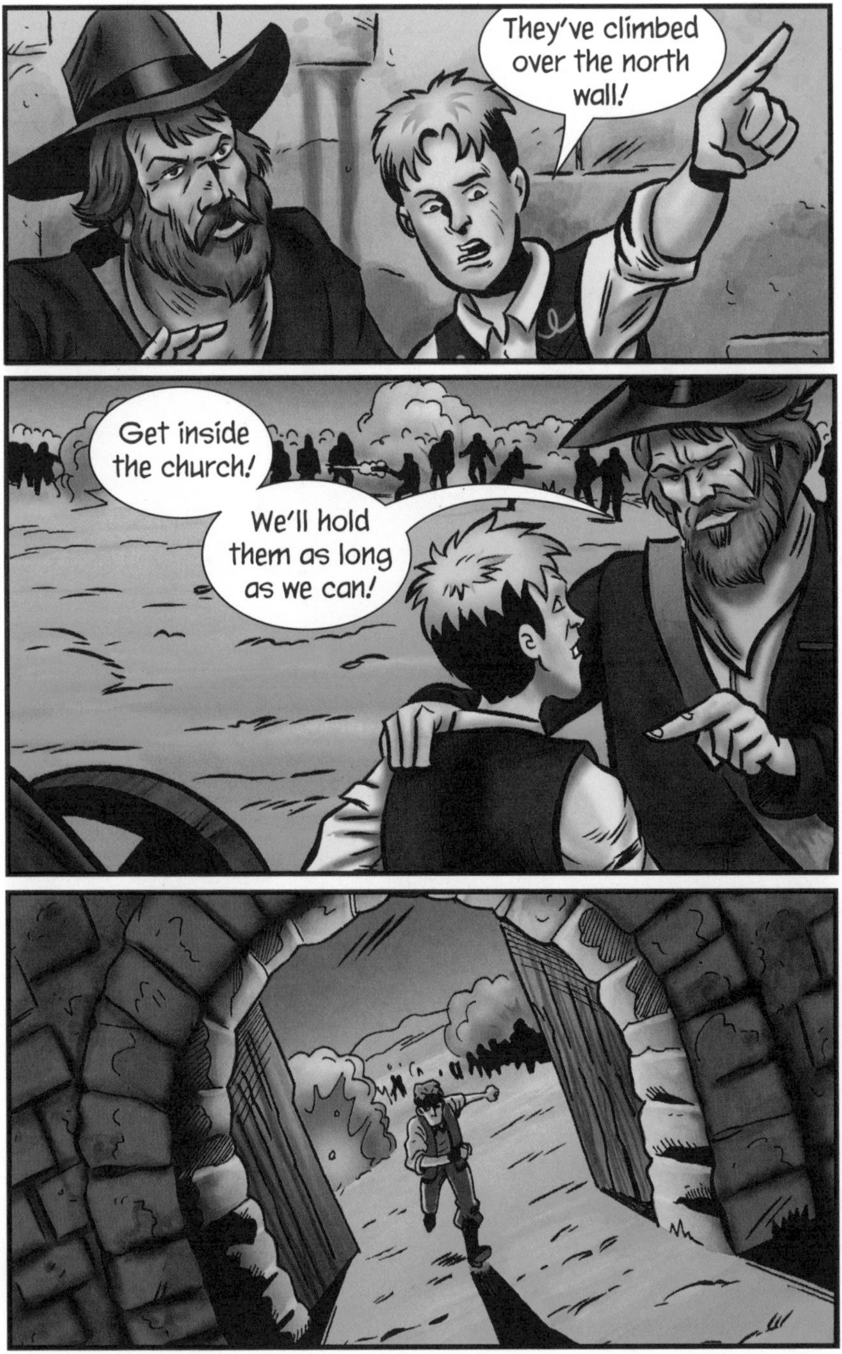
They've climbed over the north wall!
Get inside the church!
We'll hold them as long as we can!

Cal looked behind him, and the blood drained from his face. The Mexican army was breaking through the heavy wooden door.

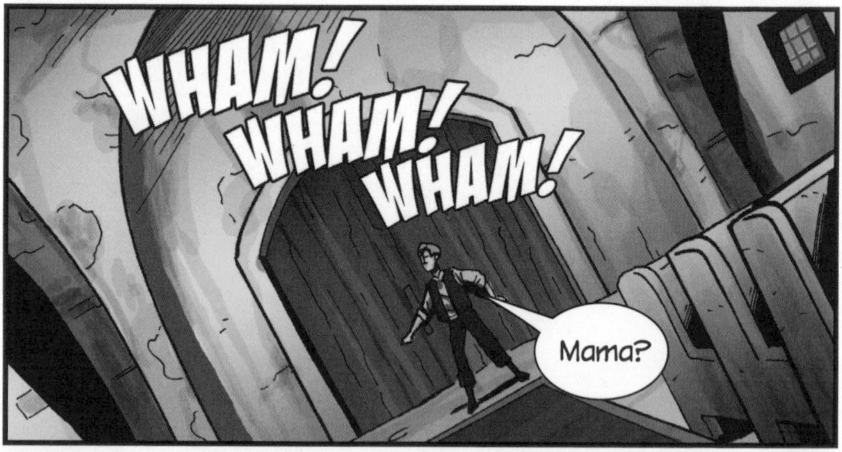
WHAM! WHAM! WHAM!
Mama?

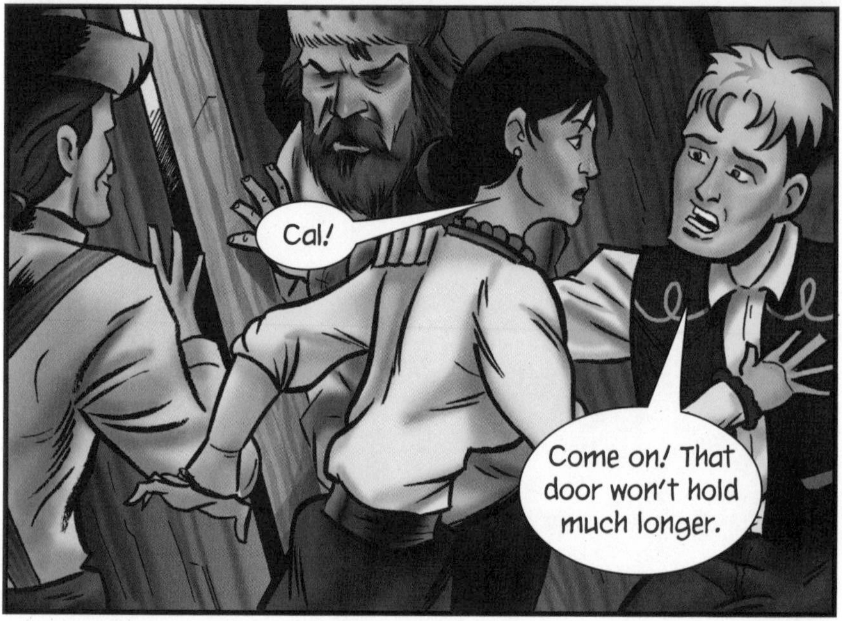
Cal!
Come on! That door won't hold much longer.

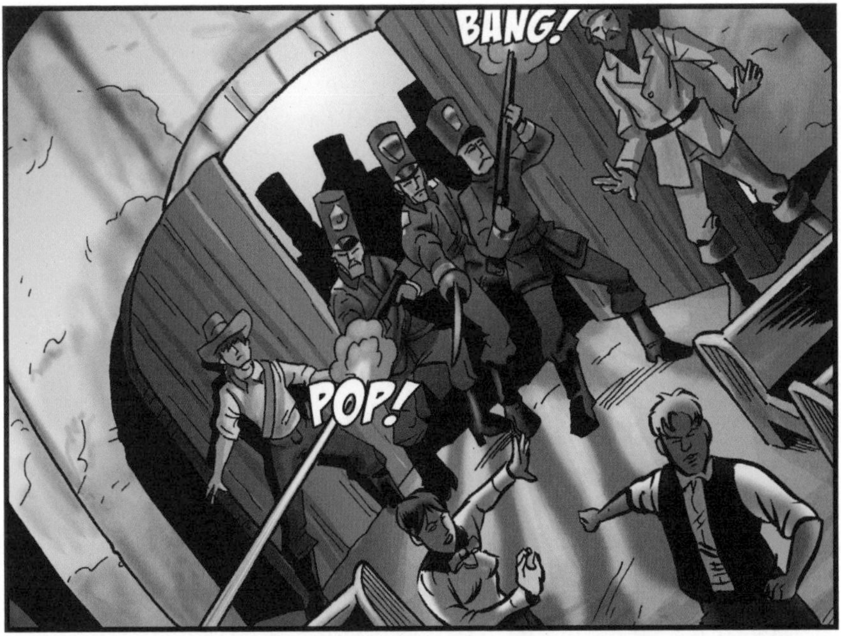
BANG!
POP!

Cal and his mother raced deeper into the mission. Behind them, dozens of Mexican soldiers poured into the Alamo, with rifles firing and swords slashing.

The defenders of the Alamo could not hold back the thousands of Mexican soldiers that swarmed the old mission. Santa Anna was set on taking over the fort. He did not want anyone in the Alamo to survive.

Cal and his mother huddled with the other women and children under a narrow archway. Together, they stood and watched as the battle continued around them. Dozens of Texan soldiers died at the hands of the Mexicans, including Colonel Travis, David Crockett, and Jim Bowie.

No matter how many soldiers the Alamo defenders fought off, more poured through the mission's doors. Cal grabbed his mother's hand. They ran deeper into the Alamo's church. Finally, there was nowhere left to go.

"Mama?" Cal whispered, no longer excited by the battle.

"Shh," Mama said, hugging Cal. She knew that she wouldn't have the answer. Neither of them knew when the battle would end. They huddled together on the dirt floor and waited.

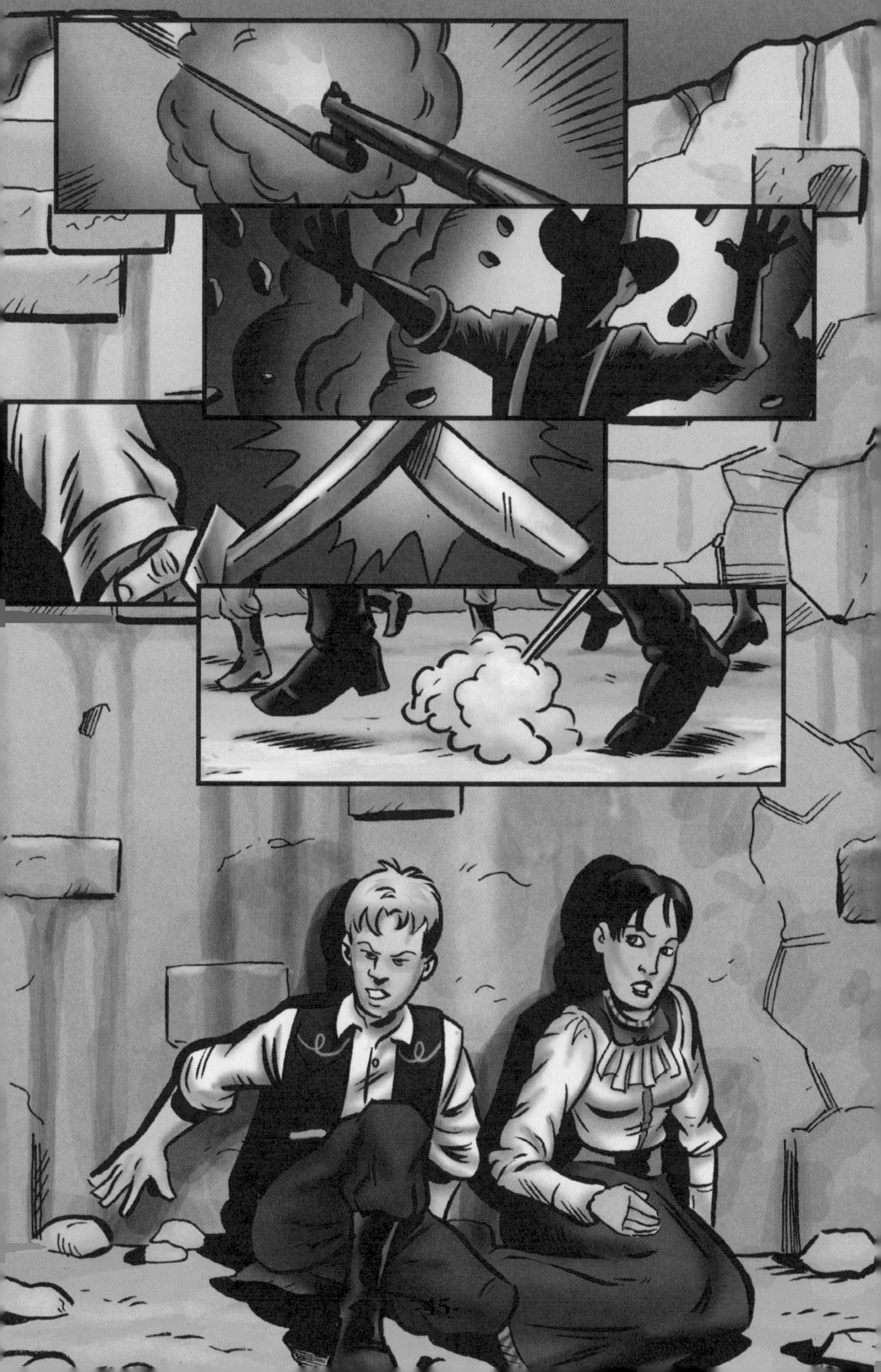

Chapter 6

REMEMBER THE ALAMO

The fighting and screaming seemed to last forever. Cal and his mother and the other women and children tucked themselves into the small archway, hoping to avoid the attention of the Mexican soldiers. Sometimes the battle found its way to them, but the Mexican army was only interested in men with weapons. Cal wondered, though, what would happen when the battle finally ended. What would happen to them?

The sounds of battle became less heated. Fewer gunshots were fired. The screams nearly stopped. Cal held his breath. He knew the battle was coming to an end. But now, they were going to be prisoners of the Mexican army.

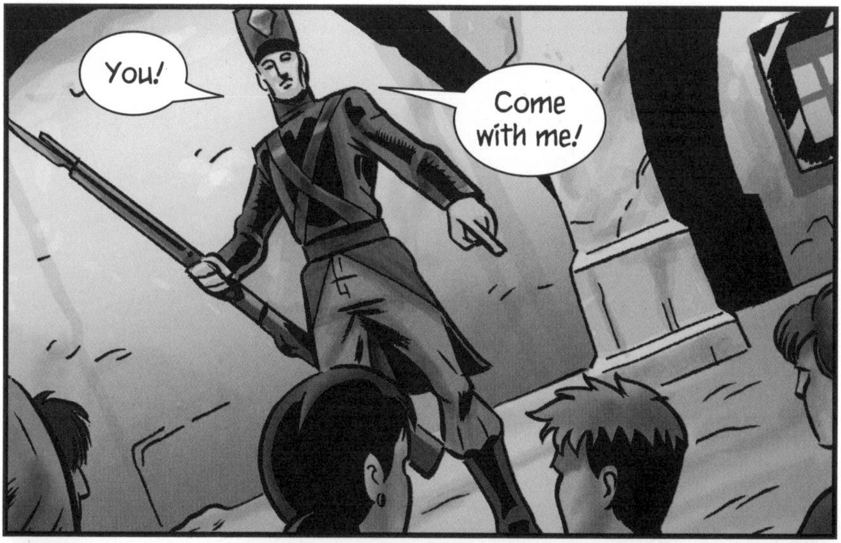
You!
Come with me!

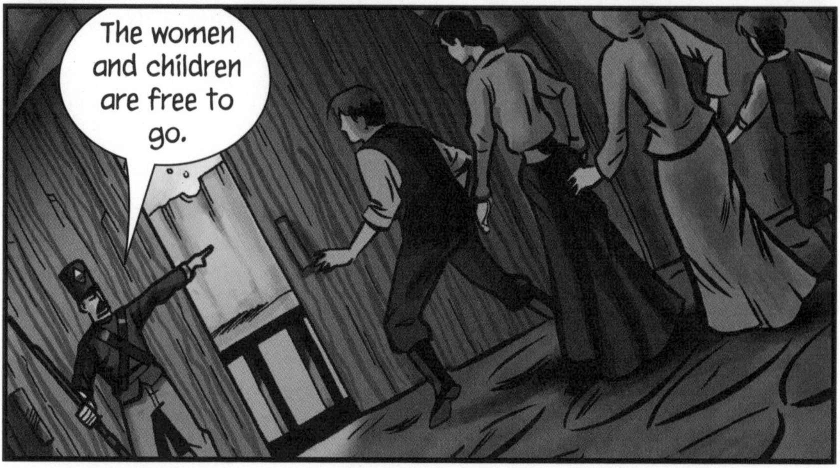
The women and children are free to go.

Cal wanted to tell the soldier that he wasn't a child. He had fought alongside the other men. But he didn't. Why had he thought battle would be a glorious thing? It was not glorious. Many good men had died.

Cal felt his mother slouch beside him. He put his arm around her to help her stand. They had been at the Alamo for nearly two weeks. The Americans may have lost this battle, but Cal knew the conflict between the United States and Mexico was not over.

Cal and his mother walked out into the bright sunshine. Even here, the ground was red with blood from fallen soldiers. Cal's skin felt dusty and sticky. Looking down at his arms, he saw splatters of blood from the soldiers that had died near him.

"It's all right, Mama," he said. "We made it. We're going home."

As Cal looked back, he remembered how the Alamo looked when they first arrived. It used to be a strong fortress. Now it was the tomb for nearly 200 brave Americans. Cal hoped no one would ever forget what happened there.

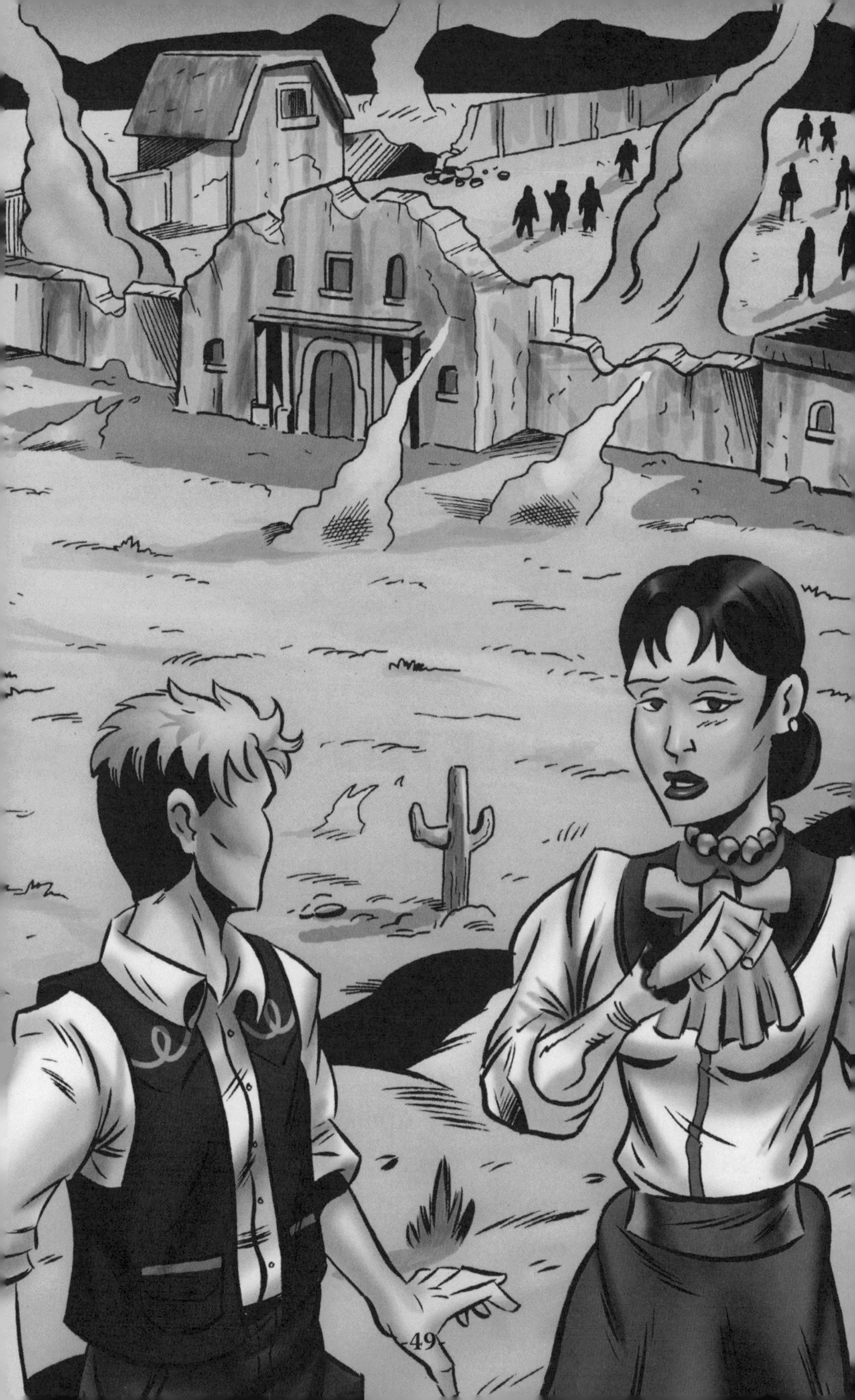

ABOUT THE AUTHOR

Lisa Trumbauer is the *New York Times* bestselling author of *A Practical Guide to Dragons.* She's written about 300 books for children, including novels, picture books, and nonfiction books on just about every topic under the sun (including the sun!). She lives in New Jersey with her husband, Dave, two moody cats, and a dog named Blue.

ABOUT THE ILLUSTRATOR

Brent Schoonover has worked as a freelance illustrator since graduating from the Minneapolis College of Art and Design in 2002. He has illustrated for companies such as General Mills, Best Buy, Target, and Continental Airlines. He also worked on several graphic novels, including *Horrorwood*, published by Ape Entertainment in 2006, and several books by Capstone Press. Schoonover currently lives in St. Paul, Minnesota, with his wife, two cats, and one bulldog.

GLOSSARY

ammunition (am-yuh-NISH-uhn)—bullets or other objects fired from a weapon

colonel (KUR-nuhl)—a military officer ranking below a general

commander (kuh-MAND-uhr)—the person in charge of a military organization or group

fortress (FOR-triss)—a place that has been strengthened against attack, such as a castle

glorious (GLOR-ee-uhss)—delightful or wonderful

liberty (LIB-ur-tee)—the quality of being free

mission (MISH-uhn)—a church or other place where religious people live and work

reinforcements (ree-in-FORSS-muhnts)—extra troops sent to strengthen a military group

strategies (STRAT-uh-jeez)—a plan for winning a military battle

surrender (suh-REN-dur)—to give up to an enemy during a fight or battle

victory (VIK-tuh-ree)—a win in a battle or contest

MORE ABOUT
THE ALAMO

During the early 1830s, Texas belonged to the Mexican government. However, more than 20,000 people from the United States had moved into the area. These people, known as Anglos, soon grew tired of following the laws of Mexican President General Antonio López de Santa Anna.

At the same time, Mexicans living in Texas, known as Tejanos, were angry with the government as well. In 1835, the Anglos and Tejanos joined together and forced all Mexican soldiers out of Texas. The Texas Revolution had begun.

Santa Anna was not about to give up Texas that easily. In 1836, he led 4,000 Mexican troops into Texas. On February 23, 1836, many of these soldiers arrived at the Alamo. About 200 Tejanos and Anglos were inside the small mission, waiting for an attack.

For the next 13 days, the small group defended the Alamo against Santa Anna's army. With few reinforcements, however, the battle could not last forever. On March 6, the men were defeated, and the Alamo fell to the Mexican army.

Historians disagree on the exact number of soldiers killed in the Battle of the Alamo. However, most agree that nearly all 200 of the Alamo defenders were killed. The Mexican army lost many soldiers as well. More than 600 of them were believed to have died in the attack. Twenty woman and children were inside the Alamo when the Mexican army arrived. All of them survived and were allowed to return to their homes.

In the weeks that followed, word of the courageous battle spread throughout Texas. On April 21, 1836, the Texan army, led by Commander Sam Houston, attacked Mexican forces near the San Jacinto river. During the battle, Houston rallied his troops by yelling, "Remember the Alamo!" In less than 18 minutes, the Texans defeated the Mexicans, captured Santa Anna, and ended the Texas Revolution.

DISCUSSION QUESTIONS

1. During the battle, Cal didn't fire a weapon. Look back through the book. What other ways did he help defend the Alamo against the Mexican army?

2. The soldiers inside the Alamo were greatly outnumbered by the Mexican troops. Why do you think they continued to fight? Do you think they should have given up? Explain.

3. What lessons do you think Cal learned from his experience at the Alamo? Use examples from the story to explain your answer.

WRITING PROMPTS

1. This story is known as historical fiction. The historical event, the Alamo battle, is true, but some of the characters are fictional. Choose your favorite historical event. Then make up a story that happened on the day of this event.

2. At the end of the story, Cal and his mother are allowed to leave the Alamo. What do you think will happen to them next? Write a story about their lives after this historic event.

3. Learn more about one of the real-life characters in this story, such as Davy Crockett, Jim Bowie, or Colonel William Travis. Write down the information you find. Then share it with others.

INTERNET SITES

Do you want to know more about subjects related to this book? Or are you interested in learning about other topics? Then check out FactHound, a fun, easy way to find Internet sites.

Our investigative staff has already sniffed out great sites for you!

Here's how to use FactHound:

1. Visit *www.facthound.com*

2. Select your grade level.

3. To learn more about subjects related to this book, type in the book's ISBN number: 9781434207531.

4. Click the Fetch It button.

FactHound will fetch the best Internet sites for you.